DEATH on the RIVER

JOHN WILSON

ORCA BOOK PUBLISHERS

Library and Archives Canada Cataloguing in Publication

Wilson, John (John Alexander), 1951-

Death on the river / written by John Wilson.

ISBN 978-1-55469-111-1

1. United States--History--Civil War, 1861-1865--Juvenile fiction.
I. Title.

PS8595.I5834D42 2009   jC813'.54   C2009-903038-1

First published in the United States, 2009
Library of Congress Control Number: 2009928872

Summary: A young soldier survives a Confederate prison camp during the Civil War.

Orca Book Publishers gratefully acknowledges the support for its publishing programs provided by the following agencies: the Government of Canada through the Book Publishing Industry Development Program and the Canada Council for the Arts, and the Province of British Columbia through the BC Arts Council and the Book Publishing Tax Credit.

Cover and text design by Teresa Bubela
Typesetting by Christine Toller
Cover artwork by Luc Normandin
Author photo by Katherine Gordon

ORCA BOOK PUBLISHERS
PO Box 5626, STN. B
VICTORIA, BC CANADA
V8R 6S4

ORCA BOOK PUBLISHERS
PO Box 468
CUSTER, WA USA
98240-0468

www.orcabook.com
Printed and bound in Canada.
Printed on 100% PCW recycled paper.

12 11 10 09 • 4 3 2 1

*For Neill, Angus and Iain
with thanks for the couch.*

JUNE 1865

ONE

I pull back the thin blanket and swing my legs over the edge of the bed. When I stand up, the tiled floor feels icy cold on my bare feet, but that's good—it reminds me that I'm alive.

There's a pile of clothes on the table by the bed. They're not mine; they were dropped off by a smiling nun who went round the ward asking if any of us needed anything. I said I wanted clothes and a pair of shoes, and her smile broadened so far that I thought her face would split. The guy in the bed beside me said he wanted his legs back, and she hurried off to help someone else.

I begin to dress, slowly because my hands are still sore. The legless guy turns his head. "Where you going?" he asks.

1

"Home," I say.

"Where's home?"

"Upstate New York," I answer as I painfully button my pants.

"That's a long way from Memphis."

I nod.

"You walking all that way?" he asks.

"Expect so."

"Lucky bastard," he says.

I pull on the shoes the nun brought. They're a surprisingly good fit.

"City shoes," the man says. "Won't last long on the road."

"I'll worry about that when I have to."

I shake his hand. It hurts, but then I'm used to pain.

"Think about me when you get blisters," he says with a bitter laugh.

"I will." I smile back.

I plan to walk north until I get home. It's not much of a plan. I've got some money, my discharge pay and a piece of paper that says that Jake Clay is no longer needed by the Union army. I'll scrounge or buy what food I can and sleep rough when I have to.

Walking all that way is a strange thing to do, but it's perfect for me. I want to go home, but I'm scared of getting there. Walking is slow enough that I can feel I'm going home but still postponing the arrival to the distant future.

At least I won't be alone.

The War between the States has been over for only two months, and the roads and rivers are clogged with men traveling in all directions. Most of them will make it home one way or another. That's the easy part. It's what you bring home inside your head that's the problem.

My hope is that the long walk will give me a chance to sort out what is going on in *my* head. Walking has always calmed me, helped me see things rationally. Maybe the miles and the dust will wear off the past I carry like a weight on my back. Make me forget the twelve months since I first went into battle that hopeless, bloody day at Cold Harbor. Make me forget the things I have seen, the things I have done, the ghosts who haunt my dreams. I can never go back to being the naïve kid I was before then, but with luck I can move forward.

I hope, but I don't know. Perhaps it's not possible to forget that you've been to Hell.

JUNE 1864

TWO

"**P**in this to my back and I'll do the same fer you."

I don't know the name of the man standing beside me in the shallow trench. I've only been a part of Baldy Smith's XVIII Corps for a few days. I arrived just in time to move up the James River to these crossroads at Cold Harbor.

"What is it?" I ask, looking at the sheet of paper he's holding.

"You're one of them new fellas that joined just afore we come up here?"

I nod.

"Ever bin in a fight?"

I shake my head.

"Well, I've bin in plenty," the man says. He's missing one of his front teeth, which causes his voice to whistle slightly as he speaks. "And this's the way it is. Soldier al'ays knows afore a battle if'n he'll be on the winnin' or the losin' side.

"Now, bein' on the winnin' side don't mean that you ain't gonna get kilt or have yer leg blowed off, but bein' on the losin' side makes it more likely, and we're sure as hell on the losin' side this day."

"How do you know?" I ask in shock. I had assumed the attack we had prepared for all yesterday would win us the battle.

The man gives me a look of pity. "What'd we do all yesterday?" he asks.

"We dug these trenches," I say.

"And disturbed the bones of a good few of the boys who fought here two years back at Gaines Mill," he says. "That weren't good luck. Where're the Rebs?"

I point through the trees into the thick dawn fog.

The man nods. "And what d'you think they was doin' yesterday?"

"Digging?"

"That'd be right. Diggin' like their lives depend on it, 'cause they surely do. Now, me and a few of the boys went forrard yesterday evenin' and saw them diggin's.

8

They got log breastworks zigzaggin' all over hell's half acre with cannons pointin' through them every few yards.

"In a couple of minutes, we're goin' over there, and as soon as we walk out of that fog, them breastworks is gonna light up like a Fourth of July picnic and there ain't gonna be space fer a mosquito 'tween them Minnie balls and canister shot. That's why we're on a hidin' to nothin' in this fight.

"Now, I plan to die facing the enemy, and I want my folks to know what happened to me. So you pin this paper with my name on it to the back of my jacket so's they'll know whose corpse it is after the fight, and I'll do the same fer you."

I feel like an undertaker, pinning the paper to his back. I notice his name: Zach Moore, written in a childlike hand.

Zach tears a page out of his diary for me to write my name on. I notice the last entry in the same scrawl: *June 3, 1864. Today I was kilt.*

For the first time I feel real fear. Not nervousness, worry or a vague sense of dread, but cold, specific, gut-wrenching terror. I can almost feel the lead balls ripping their way through my stomach and chest, shattering bones and turning vital organs to mush.

I begin to breathe rapidly and hold on to the dirt wall of the earthworks to stop from falling over.

Zach spins me around and slaps me hard across the cheek. The pain brings tears to my eyes but it gives me a focus. Gradually, my breathing calms.

"No point in becomin' a shiverin' coward," Zach says. "If'n yer time's up today, ain't nothin' you can do 'bout it. Now come on, let's get this thing done."

Zach and I clamber out of the trench and form up with the rest of the division. I feel better with others around me, especially Zach. I've only known him a few minutes, yet he already feels like a brother. I have the stupid idea that if I stay close to him, I'll be all right.

We walk forward through the trees. The sharp smell of wood smoke from a thousand campfires catches my nose. It's a comforting smell, reminding me of fishing trips back home.

The division is moving forward in grim silence, only the rattle of equipment and the occasional shouted order or curse reaching me.

We walk out of the trees, but I still cannot see the enemy fortifications through the fog. Off to my left, a roll of musket fire sounds like the clack of Mother's new Willcox and Gibbs pedal sewing machine. Then we are in the open. A flat field stretches away to another line of trees, along the edge of which the Rebels have dug in.

Zach's right—the breastworks do indeed look formidable. Rebel flags hang limp above the solid wood and earth walls, but behind them is a hive of activity. A forest of muskets, with long bayonets glinting in the rising sun, points at us, and the black muzzles of cannon are being pushed forward.

"Come on, boys," the officer in front of me shouts as he raises his sword and breaks into a rapid trot. Almost immediately, the breastworks explode in a solid wall of fire. The roar reaches me a split second later, but above it I can hear the whine of Minnie balls. Large gaps appear in our formation where canister shot from the cannons rips men to shreds. The battlefield disappears in a rolling wall of thick gray smoke.

The enemy cannot possibly see us through the smoke their cannons and muskets are throwing out, but it doesn't matter; as long as they keep on firing, they cannot miss. We hurry forward, many men hunching over as if pushing against a strong wind.

The crack of the muskets and the roar of the cannons are irregular now but still constant. We have been told not to fire our muskets until we are almost at the breastworks. Good advice, if any of us make the breastworks.

Men are falling all around. It's not as theatrical as I imagined in my childhood games. Men in battle don't usually throw their arms up, pirouette dramatically and throw themselves to the ground. Usually it's just a grunt, a sagging to the knees and an almost apologetic collapse.

Everything around me seems incredibly vivid and real. Every sight I see is sharp and every noise and smell the strongest I have ever experienced. I see a man's arm fly off and spiral slowly through the air in a red spray. I hear the soft thud of lead balls hitting the flesh of the man in front of me. I smell his blood.

I feel Zach grip my arm. I turn to see him smiling at me. A small tear in his shirt is already seeping blood. Before I can decide what to do, there is a dull cracking sound. Zach's head jerks back, his cap flies off and a small dark hole appears in his forehead. The smile is replaced by a puzzled expression, his grip loosens and he slips sideways.

"Zach?" I say stupidly as I crouch over him. He's already dead, lying on his back with blood covering half his face and his shirt front. I roll him over so that someone will see the paper on his back.

"You there. Get on."

I look up to see the officer standing over me. He's still

holding his sword in the air, but the blade is just a stump, shattered by a Minnie ball. He's not a lot older than me, but he's trying to look older by growing a mustache. It's not working; his hair is fair and his mustache looks like the fuzz on a peach. Before I have a chance to reply, the officer groans quietly and sits down.

Strangely, I don't try to help him. He has ordered me on, and that's what I do. I get up and keep going forward. I'm in a daze. I can still see and hear what is happening around me, but it's happening to someone else. I don't even care that Zach's dead.

My cap is torn away, and I feel a Minnie ball tug at my trousers. The smoke swirls and I see the Rebel lines. They are surprisingly close. I can see enemy soldiers clambering on top of them to get a better shot at us. I swing my musket around, cock it and aim at a large bearded man slightly to my right. I pull the trigger and he disappears in a cloud of smoke. I wonder if I hit him.

I rush forward and begin to scramble up the breastworks. The wood is sticky with sap, and green shoots still grow out of the fresh-cut timber. There's a man on top and he lunges down at me with his bayonet. I knock it aside and stab him in the thigh. He yells in pain and falls backward.

I only see the musket butt as a dark shape out of the corner of my eye. It catches me on the right temple. I hear a loud crack and hope it's not my skull breaking. There is a sense of falling backward into space, and then everything goes black.

THREE

I'm back home, down by the creek, at the fishing hole I used to go to with my older brother Jim. It's a beautiful calm summer day. There's barely a ripple on the surface of the deep water under the far bank where we've tried countless times to lure out the big old trout we're certain lives there. Insects are buzzing in the warm air, and a squirrel is chattering at me from the tree above.

It's a dream. I know that, but it's a good dream and I don't want to leave it.

"Stand there as long as you want. That old trout's not going to jump out of the creek into your pocket."

I turn to see Jim standing at the top of the bank, a smile playing on his face. He's three years older than me and much better looking. He inherited Ma's straight nose and high cheekbones, while I got stuck with Pa's wide fleshy face and snub nose. The girls all watch Jim go by when we go into town, and he's the favorite at the harvest dances.

In fact, everybody loves Jim, always have. When we were little, Ma would buy him candy when she went to town, and he got the better pony when we learned to ride.

"He's older than you," Ma would say. "Your turn will come when you get to be his age." But it never did. By the time I got to that age, Jim had moved on to something else and whatever it was that I was supposed to get had been quietly forgotten.

I should have resented Jim: he got everything and life was always easy for him, but I didn't. You couldn't resent Jim. I worshipped him as much as everybody else and was happy to tag along after and pick up his leftovers. And he was good to me. He didn't mind his annoying little brother tagging along and chattering aimlessly. He taught me to fish the streams and lakes all around Broadalbin and how to shoot and hunt deer in the hills above the farm. Once, he even took me the forty miles down to Albany to see the traveling diorama show about the Charge of the Light Brigade in the Crimean War.

"But there's no time for fishing now," Jim says. "We've got to get this War between the States over with first."

I glance over at the fishing hole. I can see the curved, speckled back of the trout as he swims just below the surface. It's the biggest fish I have ever seen.

"He's right there," I say, turning back to Jim. "Just one good cast will get him."

But Jim shakes his head. He's in uniform now, the smart blue one with red trim he got when he went down to Albany to join up. "I've got to go," he says cheerfully, "but don't fret. As soon as I get down there, this war'll be over before you can whistle Dixie."

I feel an immense surge of pride. "Can I come too?"

"I'm afraid not, Jake," Jim says. "You're not old enough. I'll write you though."

A movement on the stream catches my eye. The surface is covered with floating sheets of paper. I fish one out.

September 14th, 1862.
Dear Jake,

Great news. Two days back, my company came upon some Rebel pickets in a wood. I led a charge

*and cleared them out. You should've seen them run!
It was like chasing jackrabbits. Great fun and only
one boy was slightly wounded, but for it they are
going to make me a full lieutenant.*

*Imagine that, your brother a high and mighty
officer in General McClellan's Army of the Potomac.
We're heading up to a town called Sharpsburg.
That's where we'll catch Lee and chase him clear out
of Maryland and all the way back to Richmond,
you see if we don't. Then I'll come home and we'll
catch that fish.*

*Give my love to Ma and Pa and tell them
I will write longer in a couple of days.*

Jim.

I look back up at Jim. A puzzled frown has replaced
his smile, and Pa's standing beside him.

"There's been a fight," Pa says, "in a cornfield over
by Antietam Creek."

"Did Jim win?" I ask excitedly.

"Jim's still in the cornfield," Pa replies sadly.

"Why?" I ask. "If he won, he can come home now
and we can catch that fish."

Pa shakes his head, and Jim turns and walks away.
An overwhelming sense of dread descends on me.

Ma and Pa are now both standing on the riverbank. Pa looks serious and distant. Tears are streaming down Ma's face. Neither is looking at me.

"I'm here," I say. "Jim's gone, but I'm here."

It makes no difference. They won't look at me.

"I'm going to join the army," I yell. "I'll be as good as Jim. I'll be better. I won't get killed."

They still won't look at me. I have to crawl up the bank and shake them so that they see me and understand that I'm going away to the war to be as good as Jim, but I can't. Someone is holding my ankles and pulling me in the other direction.

"This'un's still alive," a voice says in a heavy southern accent.

"Well, drag him in and put him with the others," a second voice pushes its way into my dream. "The blue-bellies ain't gonna attack again tonight."

 # FOUR

I come to with a pair of Rebel soldiers holding an ankle each and hauling me, upside down, over the breastworks. I feel like my head is going to explode every time it bumps against a log. It doesn't, but I keep blacking out.

When I finally wake up, it must be the next day. I'm surrounded by about thirty other Union prisoners, most with a bloody rag wrapped around some part of their bodies. I don't recognize any of them. My head is pounding, there's dried blood all down my cheek and my right eye is almost closed from the swelling.

That morning we are forced to stagger the two miles to Gaines Mill, where we are locked in an old barn. We are held there for several days. It's hot, uncomfortable and stinks of the animals that were here before us, but it gives us a chance to recover. The pain in my head eases and the swelling goes down. There is even a water pump outside that we are allowed to use once a day, so I can clean the dried blood off my face. There's not much food, and the Rebel soldiers tease us about how easily they beat us, but for the most part, they're decent and share what food and tobacco they have.

At first I hope for another attack that might free us, but nothing happens. A few more wounded from the attack on June 3 are brought in. They all complain bitterly that General Grant didn't ask for a truce to collect the dead and wounded. It seems I'm lucky to have got so close to the Rebel lines before I was wounded. Those farther back died slowly, their screams and cries echoing across the field for days.

One morning the barn door is thrown open and a grinning Rebel officer yells: "Grant's skedaddled. We whipped you boys good. Reckon you're with us till we get to knock on Abe Lincoln's door in Washington."

I feel abandoned, but I don't have much time to fret. That morning we're formed up under guard and marched out.

For almost three weeks we travel, sometimes this way, sometimes that, sometimes held under guard in an open field for a day or two. Once we travel for three days by mule, and a couple of times we have the luxury of a train. That's where we are now, in a horse wagon on a train from Macon, Georgia. I don't know where we're headed, but I sense our journey is almost over.

"What day is it?" The soldier beside me is small, skinny and nervous. I don't much like him, but he seems to have attached himself to me and, despite my discouragements, won't leave.

"I don't know," I grumble.

"I reckon it must be near the end of the month, twenty-eighth or twenty-ninth. How much longer do you reckon they'll keep us moving?"

"Until we get where they're taking us," I reply testily.

"I heard they was taking us to a place called Belle Isle. Know where that is, Jake?"

"They're not taking us to Belle Isle," I say, angry at the kid's stupidity. "Belle Isle's in Virginia, outside Richmond. We're in Georgia and we're going in the opposite direction."

I wish the kid would shut up and leave me alone, but the harsher I am with him, the more he seems to want my approval.

"Probably a prison camp," the kid says. "We'll be all right there, Jake. I got some money." He clinks some coins in his pocket. "I'll share it with you."

I ignore the offer. It's a miracle he still has his money. I have some, but it's sewn into the lining of my jacket. Ma put it there before I left home.

"There's some rough types out there, Jake. You save this for a rainy day," she said.

I've not been in the army long, but I've learned not tell anyone about my money. The kid brags about his coins proudly to anyone who shows him the least kindness.

"How can you be so stupid?" I ask. "Sew that money into the lining of your jacket or the first person you meet will steal it."

"You're right, Jake. You're right," the kid whines. "I should've listened to you before. I'll sew it into my jacket as soon as we get somewhere. But I meant it when I said I would share it with you."

"Shut up," I order.

The kid looks crestfallen, but he falls silent. I don't want to hurt him, but he's two things I don't want right now: a friend and a distraction.

I don't want a friend because friends get killed, and I don't want a distraction because I just want to ignore everything else and think. And the more I think, the stupider I realize I have been.

I was stupid to think this War between the States was a glorious crusade for the Union and against slavery. I was stupid to think of Jim as a hero, a knight in shining armor going off to save the world. And I was most stupid to believe his letters home.

Jim must have realized what war is like—I have after only a few weeks and one major battle—but he continued writing me those cheerful, lying letters about what a big adventure it all was and how much fun he was having. Tell Zach and the others left dead and rotting in front of the Rebel breastworks at Cold Harbor how much fun war is.

Worst of all, Jim treated me like a child. I suppose he wanted to protect me from knowing what war is really like, but he didn't give me the credit of thinking I might be able to understand what was going on.

But maybe I'm being unfair. It had taken weeks of war and death for me to grow up from a farm boy, whose greatest dream was to be a hero and return home with a chest full of medals and a mind full of exciting stories, into a bitter soldier. Maybe I wouldn't have believed Jim's letters even if he had told me the truth. But he should have tried.

A change in the sound of the train's wheels makes me look up. The view past the guards and out the open door of the wagon is still mostly pine trees, but now they are thinning and I see patches of open ground and occasional shacks. We are arriving somewhere at last.

With much clanking and shuddering, the train groans to a halt. A cloud of white steam swirls past the door.

"Git down," one of the guards shouts.

Awkwardly, we scramble out of the wagon and onto the flat ground by the railroad tracks. A small station house has *Andersonville Junction* painted above the door.

"Come on, you lazy blue-bellies, form up."

With a lot of shouting and prodding with musket butts, the guards form us into a rough column. They're a lot busier and active than I have seen them before. I think it's because they are being watched by an officer on a white horse. The man is small, with narrow features partly hidden by a thick black beard. He is wearing a white, immaculately pressed linen shirt and trousers and has a gray cap pulled low on his forehead. He wears a Colt Navy revolver on his hip, but it seems ridiculously large for the man. He looks almost comical, but something about the way his eyes move, missing nothing, and the deference the guards show him make me think this is a man to beware of.

"Andersonville Junction," the kid says as we form up. "Never heard of it. You think this is where they're taking us, Jake?"

I ignore his chatter. We walk a short way along a dusty path through the trees. I'm sweating under my thick jacket. It's been an inconvenience many times as we've stumbled along under the summer sun, but some instinct tells me not to discard it. It's not going to be summer forever, and who knows where I'll be come January.

The man in front of me stops walking, and a cloud of brown dust swirls up around us. We've just come out of the trees, and as the dust clears we can see an open valley in front of us. In the center is a large rectangle surrounded by a double stockade wall. A stream runs into the stockade midway along the far side, crosses the compound and exits below us. Several neat barracks and houses are scattered outside the stockade, some surrounded by colorful gardens and low white fences.

The compound itself is crowded with tents of all sizes and shapes, and masses of dark figures move slowly between them. It is crisscrossed by a network of narrow paths.

"It don't look too bad," the skinny kid says.

I'm not so sure. The camp looks very overcrowded. The stream, clear where it leaves the trees, becomes a wide muddy mess in the middle of the compound, and off to our right there is a long shallow pit and a field of graves. Worst of all, there's a smell. It's mostly the smell of human shit, but there is an underlying sweetness that I recognize from the slaughter shed on the farm. It's the smell of death.

 # FIVE

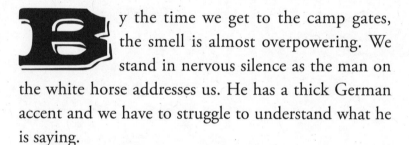 y the time we get to the camp gates, the smell is almost overpowering. We stand in nervous silence as the man on the white horse addresses us. He has a thick German accent and we have to struggle to understand what he is saying.

"Rules is simple here. Rations vonce effery day. Do not cause me no trouble and I vill not cause you no trouble. Cross ze dead line and zat is exactly vot you vill be. Ozer zan zat, do vateffer ze hell you like. Good luck."

"What's the dead line?" the skinny kid asks.

The officer nods to a guard, who steps forward. "You'll find out," he says to the kid with smile. Then he hits him hard across the cheek, knocking him down. "And you do not address Commander Henry Wirz unless he speaks to you."

"I'm sorry," the kid says miserably.

The guard kicks the kid in the ribs. "And I'm sir to the likes of you."

The double gates open and we shuffle through the two stockade walls. The kid is crying.

Inside, there is a rough open area. A crowd of ragged prisoners watches us with interest. Most seem to be staring, but I realize that this is because they are so thin that their eyes appear large in their bony faces. I am conscious that, even after the trek here from Cold Harbor, I look much healthier than most of the prisoners. I wonder how long that will last.

The prisoners move forward and mingle with us. They all want something. Some offer a place in a tent for money, others wheedle and beg for a crust of bread. One almost naked man approaches me and begins fondling the material of my jacket. I push him away and he falls over like straw figure in a strong wind.

I'm confused and sickened and, if I'm honest, more than a little scared. What is this place?

I push through the crowd and up the gentle slope, away from the disgusting stream. I need time to think, to plan what I should do so as not to end up a weak skeleton begging for scraps at the gate.

What I thought were tents from a distance are, more often than not, crude lean-tos supported by twisted, rough sticks. What tents there are are patched with scraps of canvas and torn coats.

The shelters are everywhere, and the space between them is filled with barely living men sitting listlessly or staggering about vainly searching for food. Several watch me enviously as I walk past, but no one tries to approach me.

All along the inside of the stockade wall there is an open area about twenty feet wide. It's defined by a rough waist-high fence and is overlooked by guard towers that reach above the stockade wall and are manned by bored-looking Rebel soldiers who watch my progress with little interest. I assume this is the dead line the officer mentioned. Certainly, no one seems to want to pitch their shelter too close to it, so there is a gap along the inside where the walking is easier.

Eventually, I reach a corner in the wall. This is the highest point in the camp, and I turn to survey this city of prisoners.

The shelters look even more tightly packed from here, like corpses in a huge grave, I think. The creek runs into the stockade to my left, but it is soon lost in the broad filthy swamp that is used as a toilet, as a place to collect drinking water and for washing by anyone who cares.

The smell rising from the swamp is a mixture of every horror you can imagine—death, decay, sickness and shit. It's a physical presence, catching in my throat and making me want to gag.

"Charming, ain't it?"

I look around to see a short rat-like man with a hooked nose and dark eyes standing beside me. His eyes are flickering back and forth and his hands are never still, the thin filthy fingers twisting around each other.

"Name's Billy Sharp," he says.

"Jake Clay," I say automatically.

"Pleased to meet you," Billy says, holding out a grubby hand.

I hesitate.

Billy shrugs and withdraws his hand. "No matter. Seen you at the gate is all. Thought I might help. Learn you the rules."

"Rules?"

"Al'ays rules," Billy says with a lopsided smile. "That there, for instance." He waves a hand at the fence.

"That'd be the dead line. Rule is, step over it and die."

"Why?"

"To keep us dangerous prisoners away from the stockade wall. The Rebs reckon we're so strong that if we get to the wall, we'll just rip them logs right out of the ground, kill all the guards and go off and capture old Jeff Davis and Richmond." Billy laughs bitterly. "Rules don't need to make sense; they just are, and you better learn them if you want to live."

"Why would you help me?" I ask suspiciously.

"Thing is," Billy continues, grinning widely, "ain't more'n two sorts of folk in here: them who's dead afore they know enough to stop breathin' and those, like me, who wants to live. I don't aim to end up face down in some stinkin' puddle. What sort of folk are you, Jake Clay?"

I don't trust this man as far as I could kick him, but maybe he can help me. This place is obviously a lot more complicated than Cold Harbor. There, all I had to do was obey orders, and there was only the enemy trying to kill me and me trying to kill them. Here, I suspect, from looking into the blank eyes of the prisoners around me, that the enemy might be inside my head, and I don't know how to fight him. But I do know that I have to learn quickly.

I take a deep breath of the foul air. "I want to live," I say.

"That's my boy," Billy says, slapping me on the back. "Soon as I seen you comin' through the gate, I says to mysel', 'Billy Sharp, there's one wants to live.' I can al'ays tell. Some come in here with death already in their eyes, too beat down to care anymore. They bin prisoners too long and they're just coming here to die. But then I sees a lad like yourself. Holds hisself up proud and looks around, wonderin' what sort of place this is he's landed in. That's one for the Raiders."

"Raiders?"

Billy doesn't get a chance to answer before someone stumbles against him.

The man is barefoot and dressed in rags. His brown-checked shirt is ripped from armpit to waist on one side and the right leg of his blue woolen trousers ends in tatters above his knee. The bones of the man's joints poke like knots of wood through his stretched gray skin, and his eyes, sunk deep in his skull-like face, gleam with fever. He ignores us and bends to scramble under the dead line.

"Don't," I say.

The man hesitates and looks up to see where the voice is coming from. He catches my eye and slowly shakes his head. With a painful effort he ducks, crawls under the low rail and stands up.

I glance up at the guard in the tower that rises above the stockade wall to my right. He's a kid, even younger than me. He has dark eyes that are wide with confusion as he stares at the man who has crossed the line.

"Hey, you! Get back," he yells in a high-pitched, shaky voice as he fumbles with his musket.

The man ignores the warning and steps forward.

"Stop!" the kid yells again, a note of panic entering his voice. "I swear to God I'll shoot." He cocks his musket.

I want to stop the ragged man but I'm scared to cross the dead line and face the nervous guard. In any case, what can you say to someone who has given up all hope? All I do is repeat, weakly, "Don't. Please."

The skeletal figure takes two more stumbling steps up the slope into the open, stops and stares at the ragged tops of the pine trees visible over the stockade wall. He seems unsure of what to do next.

The musket shot sounds dull, deadened by the heavy, stinking air. The man, as if exhausted by the effort of standing so long, sags to the ground, rolls gently down the slope and comes to rest at my feet.

"I'm sorry," the guard says. It sounds as if he's crying. "It's orders. I warned him."

I look down at the body in front of me. I saw men shot at Cold Harbor and I'm surprised at how little blood there is around the small dark hole in this man's chest. But then the others were fighting for life. The man at my feet welcomed death. There's a smile on his face.

As I turn miserably away, hands are already reaching under the rail, plucking at the corpse's pitiful rags. Billy follows me.

"Welcome to Hell," he says.

SIX

on't want to end up like him, eh, Jake, boy?" Billy chatters as he scuttles along behind me. I don't like Billy, but he's right. This is Hell and if I don't learn the rules, I'll end up walking hopelessly out across the dead line or lying like a vegetable in some collapsing lean-to. An unreasoning anger sweeps over me. I feel horribly cheated. I joined up to be a hero, to be like Jim. All right, war's not the way I had expected, but it's not fair that I survived the charge at Cold Harbor only to end up in this place. I spin around and grab Billy by the shirt front. "I'm not going to die here," I snarl. "I intend to survive and go home."

Billy looks startled. Then his sly smile settles back in place. "That's it, Jake. Survival's what it's all about. And I can help you do that."

"Why?"

"Man's got to have friends to survive in this place. Someone to look out for you. You watch my back and I'll watch yours. How about that, Jake?"

"What are the Raiders?" I let go of Billy's shirt.

"Mosby's Raiders. That's how we survive, Jake. See that big tent yonder?" Billy points to a large patchwork tent set up on the far side of the compound, close to the dead line where the creek runs into the camp. Now that Billy's pointed it out, I can see that the big tent, and those round about it, are cleaner and in better condition than the rest of the camp.

"That's the Raider's headquarters," Billy says. We begin walking down toward the tent. "The boss lives there. His name's William Collins, but he likes everyone to call him Mosby after that rebel raider. Story is, Collins ran his own street gang in New York. It's said he controlled all the cheap whisky and whores south of Forty-second Street."

"How did he end up here?" I ask.

"He got too big, or he didn't pay off enough of the right people. Anyways, he made powerful enemies and the gangs round him moved in to pick up the scraps. With most of his men either dead or runnin', he had to get out of there. Ended up with a gang in the Shenandoah Valley, but back in '62 that was Stonewall Jackson's territory. Collins started gettin' big ideas and callin' hisself Mosby. He says there was a battle, but I heard it weren't nothin' more'n a skirmish. Those of Collins's men who didn't run fast enough ended up here, and that was the beginnin' of the Raiders.

"Hold up." Billy thrusts his arm across my chest. "We don't want to tangle with this."

A small cart, drawn by two stumbling men, crosses the path in front of us. Its progress is followed by a chorus of curses from the people who have sprawled out onto the path and have to move to allow it by. On the bed of the cart lie three emaciated, naked corpses, their limbs flopping hopelessly over the edge with each bump.

"Dead cart," Billy says, carelessly. "There's thirty thousand men in this hellhole," he continues as we move on. "Dozens is dyin' every day. Only way to survive is to organize. That's what the Raiders do, organize. We share what we has and take care of each other. And we're al'ays on the lookout for fit young lads such as yourself to join us. How old are you, Jake Clay?"

"Eighteen," I answer.

"Eighteen," Billy repeats. He's several inches shorter than me, which means he has to look up when he speaks to me. His look is slyly arrogant and makes me feel uncomfortable.

"You must have joined up young."

"I volunteered a year ago," I say.

"Volunteered!" Billy exclaims. "Ain't no one volunteers no more, 'cept maybe a few rich folk as wants to strut in an officer's uniform back at headquarters and say they bin in a war."

Billy sniffs noisily. "Draft got me, like all the other poor slobs who ain't got the money to pay someone poorer'n them to go in their place. Why in hell'd you volunteer?"

"My older brother Jim was killed in the cornfield at Antietam."

Billy nods understandingly. "And you wanted to get revenge on them filthy Rebels."

I don't say anything. I didn't join up for revenge, but I don't want to explain my family to Billy.

"Where was you took?" Billy breaks into my thoughts.

"Cold Harbor in the Wilderness Campaign."

"That was quite the fight, I hear," Billy says thoughtfully. "Story is that old Grant left the wounded out on the battlefield to die rather'n appear weak and be the first to ask fer a truce. Was you wounded, Jake, boy?"

"I was knocked unconscious in the fight at the breastworks. Rebels pulled me in."

"You was lucky then. Me, I was taken at Chancellorsville in the spring of '63. To tell the truth, I was runnin' away from the whole bloody mess, but wouldn't you know it, I ran straight into half of Lee's army. Bin in one prison or another since, but this here's the worst."

As we head down the slope, I am continually aware of how fit, healthy and well-dressed I am compared to the average inmate. All around me, exhausted bodies lie near death, and dull eyes stare enviously at my jacket. I'll do anything not to end up like them, another member of the walking dead whose only goal is to summon up enough energy to stagger up the hill and cross the dead line. It might not be fair that I'm here, but I can't do anything about that. All I can do is swear to myself that I'll survive.

We're almost at the Raiders' tent now and the surroundings are improving. A group of healthy-looking men stand outside the entrance flap talking.

The creek water coming in under the stockade beside the big tent is muddy, but at least here it is still flowing between firm banks. Farther on, the banks disintegrate and the water barely moves through stinking black puddles.

A man steps out of one of the smaller tents, walks to the creek, drops his pants and squats. Almost immediately, a large man leaves the group, approaches the squatting man and punches him hard on the side of the head. The man falls into the water.

"What the hell you think you're doing?" the big man says. The other man struggles to pull up his pants and stand. "You know we don't foul our own nest. You need to shit, you go downstream out of our territory."

The big man punches his victim in the face once more and turns away. He notices Billy and me.

"Got a new recruit for the Raiders?" the big man asks. His head is almost square and his face shows the marks of a violent life. The eyebrows are swollen like a prize fighter's and his nose looks as if it has been broken several times. A curved, ragged scar dominates his left cheek above a scraggy growth of beard. I feel a shiver run down my spine as the man leers at me, exposing a mouthful of broken, tobacco-stained teeth.

"Yes, sir," Billy replies, standing up straighter. "This here's Jake Clay. Taken in the Wilderness and but eighteen years old. Jake, meet William Collins, the boss of Mosby's Raiders."

# SEVEN

osby takes my hand in his huge hairy mitt and squeezes. I can feel my knuckle bones grating against each other. I doubt that showing any weakness in front of this man is a good idea, so I clench my teeth and try not to wince.

"You wanna be one of my Raiders?" Mosby asks.

"I hear that's the best way to survive here, sir," I say.

Mosby nods. "That it is." He increases his grip on my hand. "There's a membership fee. How much money did you bring in?"

"Not much," I say, thinking of the six silver dollars I have sewn in the lining of my jacket.

Mosby pulls me closer until I can smell his foul breath. "That'll do then. Hand it over."

I hesitate. Mosby's face is so close I can feel his spit on my cheek when he talks. "I know a nice brought-up boy like you got something hid away, and it ain't that worthless Confederate paper.

"Now, you got a choice, Jake Clay. You can pay the fee and live safe with the Raiders. We look after our own. Ain't that right, Billy?"

Billy nods and smiles.

"Or"—Mosby tilts his head to the side at the rest of the camp—"you're free to go out there."

My hand is going numb and my jaw aches from clenching it against the pain.

Suddenly, the grip on my hand is released. I gasp with relief. Mosby moves his hand to feel the collar of my jacket.

"Mind," he says, "come winter, lots of folk here don't mind a few bloodstains on a nice warm jacket like this, and I seen men get their throats slit for a lot less."

I think back to the envious looks I received as I walked through the camp. Mosby's probably right about men getting their throats cut for a good jacket. And I suspect it's his Raiders who do most of the cutting.

"Okay," I say. I take my jacket off and rip the lining open. My hand hurts, but I ignore it and reach in to pull out the coins. They clink as I pour them into Mosby's hand.

"Welcome to the Raiders," Mosby says as all the money I own in the world disappears into his pocket. "Billy, young Jake can bunk in with you. Take him and the boys out tonight. Check out them new arrivals."

"Yes, boss," Billy says, but Mosby has already turned away.

"That was money well spent," Billy tells me as he leads the way to a small tent up the hill from the headquarters.

"It was everything I had," I say.

"Don't fret. It ain't smart to cross Mosby, and you'll get some of your money back tonight."

"What do you mean?" I ask.

We arrive at a tent. It's army issue with fewer tears and patches than many I've seen. In front of it, three men sit around a tiny fire watching a black pot of watery-looking soup.

"New tentmate, boys," Billy says cheerfully. The three men simply grunt.

"Ain't the most sociable types," Billy says with a laugh. "Grab a mess tin and have some soup."

I do as Billy suggests, and he ladles a couple of spoonfuls of thin gray liquid into my tin. There's a layer of grease floating on the top and a few unidentifiable pieces of meat lying on the bottom. It tastes oddly bitter, but I don't care. I haven't eaten anything but a couple of hard biscuits and a hunk of stale bread for three days.

"Tonight," Billy explains as he helps himself to some soup, "we go farming."

"Farming?"

Billy and the other three laugh. "Bringing in the crops," one of them says.

"Them boys that come in with you this mornin'," Billy continues. "They bin with you a while?"

"Most were taken with me at Cold Harbor," I say, "but I don't know any of them. Couple of others joined along the way here."

"Ain't none of them friends of yours then?"

On the journey here, I deliberately didn't talk to any of the others. The only one I said more than three words to was the skinny kid, and that was only because he followed me around like a lost puppy.

"No," I reply. "All my friends are dead."

Billy nods. "Friends tie a man down, and I do notice that, in this here war, they have a habit of dyin'."

"What's farming?" I ask.

"Like yourself," Billy says, "most boys who ain't been held prisoner too long got some money or valuables hid somewhere on them. Money, a watch, a pocketknife, even buttons; it's all good fer tradin'. Now you was lucky I spotted you. Mosby don't let everyone be a Raider. You get somethin' fer your money. The rest just get relieved of some extra weight."

"Robbery?"

"I prefer to think of it as gathering in the crop from the ripe plants that comes our way." One of the other men laughs coarsely. "Like I said," Billy continues, "we got to organize to survive in Hell, and the Raiders do that. You got a problem with what I'm sayin'?"

So this is the choice Mosby offered me—join his gang of thieves and live, or be thrown back into the rabble to die. Mosby frightens me, I don't trust Billy and I don't want to be a robber, but I'm scared of dying even more. The normal rules don't apply in this place.

"I don't have a problem," I say.

"Good." Billy tips up his mess tin and slurps the last of his soup. He burps loudly and wipes his greasy lips. "Can't beat a good hearty bowl of rat soup."

EIGHT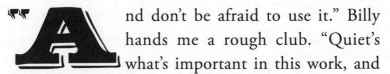

nd don't be afraid to use it." Billy hands me a rough club. "Quiet's what's important in this work, and there ain't nothin' like a gentle tap with a solid knot of hickory to quieten a troublemaker."

"Thanks," I say, hefting the club. It's not large but the dark knot that forms the head gives it a good weight.

"Personally, I prefer a blade," Billy says, running his finger lovingly along a long thin knife that glints in the moonlight.

I look around. The sky is clear and the moon almost full. All around the Raiders' part of the camp, small groups of shadowy figures are moving out.

"How do they know where the new arrivals are?" I ask.

"I weren't the only Raider that met you boys yesterday." It's light enough to see Billy's grin. "We know where most of them is bunked.

"Sam, here"—Billy waves at one of my new tentmates—"he followed one of them, looked like the sort that's got something of value stashed away."

The idea of robbery doesn't bother me too much. My fellow prisoners mean nothing to me, and if I'm to survive, I've got to live by the rules of this place. If I'm clever and lucky enough to get in with the Raiders, and others like the skinny kid are too stupid, then it's not my fault. I didn't make the rules here.

"Right, let's go. Sam, lead the way."

Even with the full moon, moving between the scattered tents and around the bodies sleeping in the open is slow work. Eventually, Sam points to a tattered lean-to on the edge of the swamp. The ground is soft here and the smell so powerful I feel the rat soup tickling the back of my throat. Billy and Sam roughly drag the two surprised occupants of the shelter out into the open. The first one out I've never seen before, but the other's the skinny kid. He stands awkwardly, trying to rub the sleep from his eyes.

"We're here from the Raiders," Billy hisses. "We don't want no trouble, so just hand over your money and we'll be on our way."

Billy is grasping the kid by the shirt. The boy is looking around stupidly. He sees me over Billy's shoulder and his eyes widen in recognition. They're blue. Why have I never noticed that before?

"Jake, is that you? What's going on?" His voice is high-pitched and too loud.

Billy slaps the boy hard across the cheek. "Keep your whinin' down if you know what's good fer you. We know you got money, so just hand it over."

"I got nothin'. Jake, tell him I got nothin'."

Billy slaps the boy again.

The kid starts crying. "I got nothin'," he blubbers. "I shoulda sewn it into my jacket like you told me to, Jake, but I didn't. Couple of fellas hustled me when I come in the gate. Took everything. You saw them, Jake."

I remember seeing the kid being jostled when we arrived. He was such an obvious target. I feel a twinge of pity. The kid's so helpless. My brother Jim always said you have to help those weaker than you. But that was a different world. This is Hell, Jim's dead and the kid's whine grates on my nerves. I'm annoyed that this isn't going smoothly.

"Give him your money, kid," I say, more harshly than I intend.

"I don't have it anymore, Jake." A track of snot runs from the kid's nose, and he wipes at it weakly with his sleeve. "They took it at the gate, like I said. I swear to God, Jake. That's the truth."

Billy's knife blade glints silver in the moonlight.

"If you want to see another sunrise," Billy says, holding the point to the kid's neck, "you'd best give us the money."

The kid jerks convulsively and Billy's blade nicks his throat, leaving a small drop of dark blood.

The kid squeals. "Oh God, I'm cut. Please don't kill me."

I step forward. This is getting out of control. The kid'll wake the entire camp. I grab his arm. "Listen," I say. "Calm down and do as you're told and everything'll be all right."

At that moment, the other man from the tent lashes out at Sam, whose attention has been focused on Billy and the kid. Sam stumbles to the side and the man breaks away and runs, crashing against tents and triggering a stream of curses. By the time Sam's back on his feet, the man has vanished.

The kid half turns and tries to pull away. "Help,"

he yells. I drop my club and grab his other arm, trying to keep him under control.

"Calm down," I repeat.

Billy moves closer.

"He's going to kill me," the kid screams. He's struggling wildly and I am having trouble holding him.

"Shut up," I snarl, frustration making me angry. "No one's going to kill anyone."

"Oh God," the kid gasps and stops struggling. Billy is up close in front of him now, and the kid is staring down between them. I let him go and move to the side.

About half the knife in Billy's hand is sticking straight into the kid's stomach. The kid is staring stupidly at the knife.

"Jake?" The kid looks up at me. His expression is an almost comical look of surprise. "Why, Jake?"

Billy takes a step forward and forces the knife hard up under the boy's ribs, almost lifting him off his feet. The kid takes in a lungful of air and coughs out a spray of blood. His surprised look vanishes as his features relax. His mouth hangs open, a thin stream of blood running from one corner. His head flops to one side, his knees buckle and Billy lowers him almost gently to the ground.

I'm in shock. It's all happened so quickly. "You killed him," I say stupidly.

Billy's already on his knees going through the kid's pockets and feeling the lining of his jacket. "Look in the lean-to," he orders. "Maybe the money's in there."

I obey automatically. There are only a couple of thin blankets. Roughly I pull them aside. There's nothing there except a creased letter. I pick it up. It's bright enough to read by the moon.

The letter's written in a neat hand.

Dearest Nathaniel,

*I hope this finds you well. Louise sends her regards. She and her mother stopped by for tea last Friday and...*I turn the letter over. It ends halfway down the page. *In hopes that this dreadful war is over soon and that you can return to your family.*

Your Loving Mother.

The kid's never going home. So what? There's thousands of boys never going home from this war. I crush the letter in my fist and hurl it angrily away.

I hear Billy curse and crawl out into the open.

"You find anything?" Billy asks.

"No," I say.

"What's goin' on over there?" I look up. There are dark figures looming out of the moonlight. "You Raiders, we've had enough of you. Your time to pay's comin'."

There are eight or ten figures and they're getting closer.

"Come on," I say, grabbing Billy's arm.

"The money," Billy says. "We got to get the money."

"Damn the money. We got to get away."

The figures are close now. I drag Billy to his feet and pull him away toward the Raiders' camp. There's no sign of Sam.

When we're safely back, Billy shakes me off. "We never got the money," he says.

"Or maybe he lost it like he said."

"Or maybe he hid it too good."

"There was no need to kill him," I say.

"His whining was gettin' on my nerves," Billy says. "Anyways, I better tell the boss we got nothin' from this one. He's not gonna be happy."

I watch Billy's retreating back and feel like bawling. Not because the kid's dead and his mother'll miss him. Life's pitifully cheap in this place. What's tying a knot in my gut is that, in all the time the kid and I were together, I never knew his name was Nathaniel.

 # NINE

It's already noon the next day, but I'm still in the tent, too exhausted and miserable to move. I haven't slept a wink. Every time I close my eyes all I can see is the surprised face of the kid Nathaniel, as Billy sticks the knife into him.

Billy doesn't care. His only worry is that we didn't get any money and that Mosby will think we stole it. Billy doesn't understand how I feel.

"He would've been dead in a couple weeks anyway," he tells me. "Dozens gets dragged out to the grave every day. He's just one more loser, didn't have what it takes to survive in here. Forget him."

But I can't forget him, and I don't understand, any more than Billy does, why Nathaniel's death bothers me so.

The deaths I saw at Cold Harbor don't worry me—I can't even remember what Zach looked like—but the kid's haunts me. I know I was partly responsible, I held him while Billy stabbed, but I didn't do it deliberately. I was trying to calm him.

Maybe it's because the kid was so weak and helpless. Nathaniel just wanted to live and didn't know how to. He never stood a chance against the likes of Mosby and Billy—or me.

I'm a Raider now, one of the strong, one of the killers. But I don't want to change that just because I feel bad about the kid's death. Being one of the Raiders also makes me one of the survivors, and I want to live. I don't feel bad enough about last night to want to go and sit beside the stinking cesspool of the creek. Besides, what good would starving to death do? It wouldn't bring Nathaniel back. I've made my choice, to live at whatever cost. I just wish I didn't feel so shitty about it.

"What's going on? Who the hell are you?" Mosby's voice breaks into my self-pity. It's loud and angry enough to make me crawl out of the tent to see what's happening.

Mosby and a few others are standing outside the big tent. Several are holding clubs, knives or brass knuckle-dusters. Mosby's shouting at a group of about a hundred men from the rest of the camp.

A jolt of fear runs down my spine. My first thought is that these men are here for Billy and me. That they want to avenge Nathaniel's death. I'm certain that Mosby will hand us over as quick as blink if he thinks it'll be to his advantage.

"We're Regulators," a tall skinny man at the front replies. "We've had enough of your Raiders and their murdering ways." A rumble of agreement runs through the group. "We're here to arrest you."

"Arrest me?" Mosby grins. "I run this camp. Ain't no bunch of ragged do-gooders goin' to change that. Even if you do have a few sticks. Now get back to your hovels and maybe I'll forget this."

"We can't do that," the thin man says.

Mosby takes a step forward but stops and looks over at a disturbance by the main gate. A squad of Confederate soldiers is coming in. Prisoners scramble to get out of their way as they head over to us and form a ragged line on each side of the Regulators. They cock their muskets and level them at Mosby and the others by the big tent.

"You see," the leader of the Regulators continues, "we talked with Commander Wirz, and he agrees that something needs to be done about your murdering gang. Now, if you come quiet, you'll get a proper trial with lawyers and such. If not—" The man gestures at the armed soldiers.

Mosby stares hard at the Regulators, an expression of cold fury on his face and his shoulders tensed for action. The future hangs in the balance. If Mosby gives the word, there will be a bloodbath and my plan of surviving as a Raider will be destroyed.

Mosby's shoulders relax and he laughs. "All right. We'll come quiet. I'll wager I can afford a better lawyer than you." He turns to his cronies around him. "Come on, boys, let's play their game."

The Regulators move forward and begin rounding up the Raiders. I stare at the men moving toward me. In twenty-four hours, I have gone from being a confused new prisoner, to a privileged Raider, to a criminal without even the chance of life I came in with. I've lost all my money and am feeling hideously guilty about being part of murdering a helpless boy. Any control I had of my life has vanished.

"Jake! There you are." I look round to see Billy coming toward me. "What'n hell you doin' in the middle of the Raiders' camp?"

I stare at Billy in confusion. The two Regulators who are approaching me stop.

"I told you not to come here on your own. You ain't gonna get your money back."

"Who're you?" one of the Regulators asks.

"Name's Billy, and this here's Jake. We come in yesterday. Been walking for weeks, ever since we was captured at Cold Harbor."

"Why're you in the Raiders' camp?"

"That'd be Jake's fault," Billy says with a smile. "Raiders came to our tent last night. I got nothin' to steal, but Jake here had some coin stashed away in his jacket. The scum took every cent. Show these boys the rip in the linin', Jake."

I open my jacket and show the torn place where my money was.

"Now, Jake, he ain't one to take that sort of thing lyin' down. Are you, Jake?"

I shake my head blankly.

"So, this mornin', Jake says he's comin' over here to get his money back. I says don't be stupid. Just get yourself beat up or worse if you come into this hornet's nest and start causin' a ruckus. But Jake's a stubborn sort and he snuck away while I weren't lookin'. Just as well you lads come along afore he got himself into a real mess. Now, we'll just go and get Jake's money and be on our way."

"Can't let you do that," the Regulator says. "We got orders to collect all the valuables we find and hold them. If you boys got a claim, you take it up after the trial with the judge."

Billy scratches his ear, thoughtfully. "Well, I suppose that's fair enough. What do you say, Jake?"

"Fair enough," I say.

"Least there won't be Raiders to bother honest folk anymore. Mighty obliged to you boys."

Billy takes my arm and leads me away from the Regulators. They don't try to stop us. We walk in silence until we are well clear of the Raiders' camp. He sits down and starts laughing.

"I'll be damned," he says eventually. "Those boys finally got some backbone. You're lucky I was close by and thinkin'."

"Thanks," I say.

"I didn't do it just for you," Billy says. "It was the easiest way I could see to get both of us out of there."

"What'll happen now?" I ask.

"Way I see it, Mosby gets a good enough lawyer, swings the trial and comes back to start up again, or else they hang him. Either way, the Raiders as we knew them is gone, and we keep a low profile for now."

"Won't be too hard," I say. "We've got nothing."

"Don't be so sure." Billy smiles and shakes his pocket. I hear the rattle of coins. "I got a little put aside fer a rainy day like today. And I got this." Billy shows me his blade. "We're survivors, Jake, you and me.

Not like them weaklings that don't last a day in here. We'll get by."

"Why are you helping me?" I ask.

"You think I would desert my friend?"

"Billy, if it was to your advantage, you'd feed your mother to a pack of coyotes."

Anger momentarily flashes across Billy's face. Then he laughs again. "You got me pegged, Jake, boy. Remember what I said about the way to survive bein' to organize? Well, I want us to be a team. With Mosby out of the picture, maybe permanent, you and me is the Raiders, at least fer now."

TEN 👉

It takes Billy and me two days to get a shelter.

"Got to find a small one with only a couple of men in it," Billy says. "Make sure at least one of them's sick. Then we move close by and wait, so's we're the first to move in when they die."

"That could be a long wait," I say.

Billy winks at me. "Less'n you might think. Most folk's ain't got a long life expectancy here."

We split up and wander around the camp. It's even larger and more crowded than I thought when I arrived. Billy says it's something like sixteen acres, although you lose a couple of acres of living space for the swamp in the middle. According to the roll call we have to attend every day at 7:00 AM, there's more than thirty thousand men in that space.

It's hard to tell exact numbers because the roll call's pretty chaotic. Most prisoners are divided into detachments of about a thousand men each. Within each detachment, men naturally try to keep the army structure together, cavalry stick with cavalry, Pennsylvania regiments stay close and so on. The groupings within the detachment often call themselves "regiments," but they vary in size and, as there are few officers in here, they are run by sergeants. Each detachment is counted separately, but the guards are often lazy and simply accept the figures that the sergeants give them. In addition to the detachments, there are what the Rebel guards call floating prisoners, not part of any group. Most prisoners try, through a false sense of security, to join a detachment, but some, like Billy and me, are happy enough to be independent.

"I don't want to be beholden to any sergeant who thinks he's good enough to be an officer," Billy says. "Only advantage I can see of this place is a chance to get out from under that army discipline."

At best the count at roll call is just a rough estimate, and it doesn't take account of the men too sick to leave their shelters. The only truly accurate count is of the bodies taken out for burial every day.

On the second day of looking, I find our shelter. It's up near where I first met Billy. It's a lean-to but sturdy, and the patched canvas looks as if it would keep out all but the heaviest rain. Best part is, of the two men outside it, one of them's already dead.

The living one looks like the pictures I've seen in my schoolbooks of an Old Testament prophet. He's almost naked, wearing only cutoff trousers and a patched jacket that still sports half a dozen shiny brass buttons. He has filthy, matted hair and beard and wild staring eyes, and his skin has a yellowish tinge. He's squatting, rocking back and forth beside his tentmate, mumbling to himself. I rush off to find Billy.

By the time we get back, the dead cart's there, but the wild man won't let them take the body.

"Angels is comin' to take him," the man screams, clutching onto his tentmate's legs as the dead-cart men haul on the other end. "This is Hell and death is a release. I told him the angels would take him to Heaven. Here they come." The man throws his head back, and everyone within hearing looks up.

There's nothing there, just a few white clouds scudding across the blue.

"Let go, you crazy old coot," one of the dead-cart men says. "Ain't no angels in this place." The two men give one last tug and release the body. The wild man collapses, sobbing on the ground. As the dead cart rumbles off, Billy steps forward.

"Don't show no respect in this place," he says. "That a close friend?"

The man looks up, his tears cutting two tracks down the filth on his cheeks. "My brother," he says. "They wouldn't leave him. The angels is comin', fer sure." I had assumed that the man was old, but up close I can see that, beneath the dirt, he's not more than a few years older than *my* brother Jim.

"Angels'll find your brother wherever he is," Billy says soothingly.

"No!" The man yells and lurches to his feet. "I spoke to them direct. Told them to come here. Now they'll never find him. We're all trapped in Hell."

"Calm down," Billy says. "It'll be fine. How'd it be if me and Jake here build a fire and boil some water?"

"You're the devil," the man says, swinging a fist weakly at Billy. Billy dodges easily and the man falls over. "You want to tempt me from the path of righteousness. The angels is comin' to Hell, I say, but they ain't comin' fer the likes of you." He looks slyly up at us. "And you want my tent. You can't have it. It's fer the angels." He crawls back into his lean-to and huddles in the shade.

"What do we do now?" I ask.

"We wait," Billy says. "Ain't gonna be long."

That night we sleep on the ground near the crazy man's lean-to. I'm troubled by strange dreams.

Nathaniel's there, staring accusingly at me, but so is Jim, standing beside him. They're both surrounded by glowing white angels. One of the angels has the bearded face of the crazy man. He's smiling.

"You want to kill me," he says, "but my angels won't let you. Will they, Jim?"

My brother steps forward. "No more killing. If the strong don't protect the weak, we're no better than animals. You must make amends, Jake, amends."

"How?" I ask, but no one answers. They just stand there and laugh. Jim's face has changed to Billy's. "Survive. Do what you have to. Live," he says gleefully. "The strong survive, the weak die. That's the way the world is."

I wake up sweating and confused. Clouds are covering the moon and it's dark. I roll over to get more comfortable on the hard ground. I notice that Billy's gone. To the latrines, I suppose. I drift back into my disturbed sleep.

ELEVEN

ake up, Jake, boy." Billy shakes my shoulder. "We got oursel's a shelter."

I sit up and rub my eyes. I have a pounding headache and I don't feel as if I've slept at all.

"What?" I ask stupidly.

"We got oursel's a shelter. The old coot died in the night. Come and help me get his body out. We got to let everyone know this place is ours afore we go down to roll call and rations."

"Died? What did he die of?"

Billy laughs. "What does anyone die of in this place? It weren't old age, that's fer sure. Now come and help."

66

Together we haul the body out of the lean-to and lay it beside the track for the dead cart. The man looks peaceful.

"I hope his angels come for him," I say.

"Angels! Ain't no angels here fer the livin' nor the dead. All there is is us, and all we can do is the best we can to survive. Start believin' in angels and you ain't gonna last long.

"Well, I'll be. Look at this."

Billy has been rummaging among the blankets in the lean-to. He sits back, holding up a small black bag. He rattles it, and I hear the clink of coins.

"We struck it lucky, Jake, boy. He may have been crazy, but he knew enough to keep something aside. And we got ourselves some good blankets, a flint, a couple of mess tins, a pocketknife, a watch, and there's even two forks in here. We're gonna live like kings."

Billy stands up and addresses the men in the tents around us. "The crazy coot's dead now, as dead as his brother was yesterday."

"How'd he die?" someone shouts.

"In his sleep," Billy answers. "Reckon his angels came fer him after all."

"Dead from a blade between his ribs, more like," the man outside the tent nearest us says.

"This blade?" Like lightning, Billy whips out his knife, steps over and holds it under the man's nose.

"I didn't mean nothin'," the man says, drawing back. "Don't care what the fool died of."

"No," Billy says, "we got to clear this up. I ain't about to have folks whisperin' that me and Jake come by this place foul. I'll make a deal. You check the body and if you find a knife hole, you can have my blade, and me and Jake'll go and find ourselves another shelter. If'n you don't find no hole, you shut up."

"It's okay," the man says nervously. "I believe you."

"But others might not now that you've put the suspicion in their minds. Check."

Reluctantly, the man goes over to the body and checks it for knife wounds. The rest of us watch in silence. I'm remembering that Billy was gone when I woke in the night.

"Aint nothin' there," the man says, straightening up. "Must've died in his sleep like this fella says."

Billy nods. "Ain't good to have distrust 'tween neighbors. Now we can all look out fer each other."

"Sure," the man says.

Billy goes to the body and deftly slices off the brass buttons from the dead man's jacket. He tosses one over to our neighbor.

"There," he says, "that'll get you some wood fer a fire."

"Thank you," the man says in surprise.

"'Tain't nothing," Billy says with a smile. "Just bein' neighborly. Come on, Jake. Our spot'll be safe enough now. Time we was at roll call."

On the way down the hill, I wonder how the crazy man really died. Billy had put the thought in my mind, and stabbing is not the only way to kill a man, especially a sick, weak one. But I push the thought away. We have a shelter and blankets now.

Roll call is more cursory than usual this morning, and the guards seem nervous. We are given our half-brick-sized piece of corn bread and, as if to confirm that this day is different, a rare slice of salt pork. Just after we've grabbed our share, there's a commotion at the gate. The guards stand to attention and Commander Wirz rides through on his white horse, dressed exactly as he was the first time I saw him.

"Death on a pale horse," a man beside me whispers.

Wirz sits for an age and surveys his pathetic charges.

"I haf examined ze Raiders," he says eventually. "Zey are, as you say, bad mens. But zere are too much of zem. I shall keep ze six baddest for you men to try, and at vun of ze clock today, I shall return ze rest."

A rumble of complaint rises from the men, but Wirz ignores it, turns his horse and rides out the gates.

"What does he mean?" I ask Billy.

"The Regulators must have taken more than a hundred Raiders. I reckon old Wirz don't want the trouble of lookin' after them or decidin' what to do with them, so he's just throwin' them back and keepin' the six worst so that he can claim he's doin' somethin'. Word is, he's already got lawyers and such, and a jury of new men all lined up. At least it should be some entertainment this afternoon."

I sit for the rest of the morning chewing thoughtfully on the coarse corn bread. It gives my stomach cramps, which are eased if I eat slowly. The salt pork I wolfed down before I was even halfway back to our shelter. Billy is off somewhere.

I'm confused. On the one hand, I'm doing well. I have a shelter, I'm fitter than most of the men in Andersonville and I'm sure Billy and I can survive one way or another. On the other hand, my dreams are getting more complex and disturbing. And what if Billy had killed the crazy man last night; will that be something else on my conscience?

But it's Nathaniel who really bothers me. Nathaniel and Jim. Jim would never have let Billy kill the kid.

But I'm not Jim, and Jim never knew what Hell is like. Decent human beings don't live long here. You have to be tough to survive, and I aim to survive.

"Come on, stop moping about. The fun's about to start." Billy slaps me on the shoulder and stuffs a bundle of sticks inside the lean-to.

"Where did you get that?" I ask, pulling myself out of my self-pity.

"Traded the crazy man's buttons fer it," Billy says with a smile. "Now come on, they're about to let the Raiders back in, and the Regulators got a welcome party fer them."

All the way down I want desperately to ask Billy if he killed the crazy man last night, but I say nothing. I want even more *not* to know. That way, the ghosts in my dreams can't blame me.

Most of the camp is assembled on the hillside by the main gate to see what happens when the Raiders are let back in. Billy and I find a spot near the dead line where we have a decent view.

The Regulators, and some who just have a grudge against the Raiders, form two long parallel lines stretching away from the gate. Everyone has a weapon—usually just a rough stick, but many have vicious-looking clubs that I suspect used to belong to the men who are about to have to run that gauntlet.

We wait for a long time as the anticipation mounts for either vengeance or a spectacle to break the boredom. Eventually, the gates are thrown open and, one by one, the Raiders are forced into the compound.

The first man, a large brute with a face that's been in many fights already, takes a moment to realize what is expected of him, spits derisively, puts his head down and runs forward. The clubs and sticks rain down, but the man keeps going. Many of the stick-wielders seem intimidated by the man's size and contempt, and hold back or only hit weakly. The man staggers and falls twice, but each time he gets up and continues. At length, bloody and bruised but still defiant, he reaches the end.

The next man is small and skinny. He looks horrified at the spectacle facing him and begs to be let go.

"I didn't do nothin'," he pleads. "I weren't no Raider."

"Yes, you were," a man in the line shouts. "You and Mosby stole my watch. Beat me unconscious. It's your turn now."

The skinny man, encouraged by the guards' bayonets, starts off down the line. He doesn't run fast and moves from side to side, increasing the distance he has to cover. He's down before he's gone ten yards. He struggles to his feet and pleads with his attackers to stop. His screams and his weakness just seem to encourage the crowd and they attack him with much more vigor than the big man.

The skinny man goes down four more times. The last time he doesn't get up, just lies there, curled into a ball with his hands over his head, letting the blows rain down. I hear a loud crack, which is probably a bone in his arm breaking. He's not even screaming anymore.

Another man is pushed through the gate, and the crowd's attention is focused on him. The skinny man manages to crawl through the surrounding men's legs and escape.

So it goes on all afternoon. Some men race down the middle, others try to break through the lines at each side. I count a dozen men who are beaten senseless and at least three who are probably dead.

Occasionally Billy whispers a man's name, but the only one I recognize is his old tentmate, Sam. He runs hard, cursing loudly as he goes, and escapes with not too severe a beating.

Men drop out of the lines from exhaustion, but there are always others ready to pick up their bloody clubs and continue. Oddly, the crowd's greatest fury is focused on the weakest. They seem to hold back when a large defiant man runs between the lines, but if someone shows the least weakness by pleading or whining, they show no mercy and go at him like a pack of wild dogs.

"Glad I weren't part of that," Billy says after the spectacle is over and we are heading back to the shelter.

"It was brutal," I agree.

"But 'tain't nothin' to what they'll do to Mosby and the other five. They best hope Wirz and his lawyers and jury decide on a hangin'. Least that'd be a quick end."

JULY 1864

TWELVE 👉

It's hangin' day." Billy sounds almost gleeful at the prospect. "Won't be long now."

I scratch at the latest crop of louse bites and crawl out into the morning air. Soldiers and prisoners always have lice, but the crazy man's blankets and lean-to are louse heaven. Ever since Billy and I moved in, we've been eaten alive. We've killed hundreds of the little blood-engorged creatures by running candle flames along the seams of our clothing or just holding our shirts and pants over the fire. The lice make a satisfying crackling pop, but there are always thousands more. We try not to scratch our skin raw, but the itching is unbearable.

I look over the compound. Across the swamp, a gang of prisoners is busy putting the finishing touches to a scaffold. It's a simple affair: a long stout beam has been set up about fifteen feet above the ground and six noosed ropes thrown over it. Below the nooses, a narrow platform made of two planks spans the distance between the uprights that support the beam. The planks are balanced on wooden cleats notched into the uprights. A crude set of steps leads up to the platform.

Men with hammers stand beneath the platform, one on each side. When they knock the cleats out, the platform will drop and so will anyone standing on it—at least as far as the rope around their necks will allow.

Mosby and the other five have been found guilty and sentenced to death. The trial was held outside the compound, but the men had lawyers selected from among the prisoners. Every day there was a line of men at the gate waiting to give evidence of what crimes they say Mosby and the others committed. By rights, I should have been with them, testifying about what happened to Nathaniel, but that would just put Billy on the scaffold with the others and then I would be alone.

The jury was made up of men recently arrived by train. The idea is that they will not be biased, but every evening they are sent back into the compound, where they are surrounded by prisoners seeking news of the trial and where the Regulators make sure they know exactly what will happen if they don't find Mosby and the others guilty. The trial finished yesterday, July 10, and today is hanging day.

"Wonder what'll happen to all that good timber after they string them up?" Billy ponders.

"Do you think the Raiders will try and stop the hanging?" I ask.

"If they're real stupid, they might," Billy says.

"Stupid? There's a hundred of ex-Raiders in the camp. Enough to overwhelm the guards at the scaffold."

"Look." Billy points to the hillside up by the train station.

I haven't looked outside the stockade, but Wirz has been busy. All along the tree line, he has set up cannon facing down into the compound.

"I'll wager those guns is primed with canister shot and grape," Billy goes on. "If there's a general riot, which there surely will be if the Raiders try anything, Wirz'll give the order to fire. Least it'll solve the overcrowding." Billy laughs harshly.

Quite a few local families are arriving on the hillside and setting up picnics where they can look in at us and the hanging. It's almost a festive occasion.

A commotion at the gate distracts me. The men are being led in, surrounded by armed Rebel guards and followed by Wirz on his white horse. The crowd surges forward amid shouts of "Hang them!" The guards force a way forward.

Mosby looks completely unconcerned, glancing around and waving to friends in the crowd. The other five look terrified, staring wild-eyed at the scaffold.

All of a sudden, one of the condemned men bursts through the line of guards and runs down the hill. He pushes surprised spectators aside and crashes through tents and lean-tos.

I glance nervously up at the loaded cannons pointing at us and hope the officer up there is calm.

The escapee doesn't get far. He keeps just ahead of his pursuers until he arrives at the swamp. He plunges in, but sinks up to his thighs. A couple of Regulators grab him, hit him a couple of times and drag him back to the line.

"Be a man," Mosby shouts at him and the others. "Did you think you was goin' to live forever?"

At the foot of the scaffold the procession stops and Wirz addresses the crowd.

"Here iz your men back, as I found zem. I have nossing more to do viz zis and vash my hands. Do viz zem az you vish." He turns his horse and rides out of the compound, followed by the armed guards.

The crowd lets out a low moan and surges forward.

"They're gonna tear them apart," Billy says under his breath.

But the man who led the Regulators to the Raiders' camp climbs onto the scaffold steps.

"Easy, boys. We want this done right. These men are guilty as hell and we have the trial to prove it. Now, we are prisoners, but we are still Union soldiers and we'll act as such. Much as you all want your pound of flesh from these devils, we must hang them according to law. We ain't savages."

This calms the crowd somewhat and they allow the men to be led up the steps. The legs of the man who ran don't seem to be working too well and he has to be almost carried up.

Eventually, the six are lined up on the board beneath the hanging nooses. A chaplain climbs up and begins reading something about leaving the cares of this world behind and preparing for the next, but no one pays him much attention.

"Any last words, boys?" the Regulator leader asks cheerfully.

Mosby remains silent, but the others shout out for mercy and forgiveness. All they get in return is abuse and curses. The man who had tried to run is sobbing uncontrollably and pleading for his life.

"I hardly done nothin'," he says.

"You slit my brother's throat for twenty dollars, you filthy scum," a man in the crowd shouts to a roar of approval.

"Enough," the leader says.

Six men step forward and tie the condemned men's hands behind them. Then they slip coarse cornmeal sacks over their heads, slide the nooses down and tighten them. Everyone but the six leaves the scaffold.

The crowd is silent, the only noise being the muffled sobbing from some of the men on the board.

The men below hammer on the cleats and jump out of the way, the platform falls and, accompanied by an involuntary gasp from the crowd, the six figures drop.

What happens next startles everybody watching. The drop is apparently not enough to break anyone's neck. Five men strangle slowly, kicking and twisting grotesquely. The sixth, Mosby, proves more than his rope can bear and with a sharp snap he lands in a crumpled heap on the ground. Two men run forward, undo the noose and tear off the meal-sack hood.

"He's out cold but he's still breathing," one shouts.

"Bring him round and do it again," the leader commands.

The crowd's restless. They hadn't expected this. I hear voices behind me saying, "It's a sign" and "He ain't meant to die."

Water is thrown in Mosby's face and he opens his eyes.

"Where am I?" he asks groggily. "Is this Heaven?"

"You're still in Hell," someone shouts.

Mosby looks up at the still struggling bodies of his companions and the beam where two men are busily rigging up a new noose.

"Oh Christ, boys, don't put me up there again." All Mosby's previous composure is gone. The man who terrified and murdered so many is a blubbering wreck, tears and snot pouring down his face, his neck raw from the first hanging. "God has spared me. Be merciful, please."

"God may not want him," someone to my right shouts, "but Old Nick's stoking the fires and sharpening his pitchfork. Make the rope strong this time, boys."

A few men laugh nervously.

Mosby's lifted back up onto the board and the new noose and meal sack placed over his head. He never stops sniveling and begging for mercy, even after his voice is muffled by the hood.

This time the rope doesn't break and Mosby hangs, twitching beside the others.

With the entertainment over, men begin to drift away, but Billy makes no move. I look at him. He's staring, wide-eyed, at the bodies turning slowly in the afternoon breeze.

"You all right?" I ask.

Billy shakes his head as if to clear it. "Ain't never seen a hangin' afore," he says distantly. He turns to me. I've never seen him so serious. "I ain't got but one fear in this world and that's drownin'. Near enough the only memory I got of my daddy afore he drank hisself to death is the time our dog had pups.

"She weren't much of a dog, scrawny mutt with fleas, but I certainly loved that dog. When she had six pups, I thought we'd have a whole pack of dogs, but weren't to be. One day my daddy took me and the pups down to the creek. Made me watch as he drowned the lot of them. I was cryin' and screamin' at him to stop, the pups were squealin' and the old dog was whinin' somethin' fierce, but Daddy just kept goin'. He drowned them one by one, holding them under until they went limp. I could almost feel them little things strugglin' to breathe with nothin' but water all around.

"Ever since that day, I've had a mortal terror of drownin'."

"Why is that bothering you so today?" I ask.

"Because it struck me, watchin' Mosby and the boys twitchin' on the end of their ropes, that hangin's much like drownin', locked in the darkness of that hood with no air to be had. And I know well enough what wrongs I done in this place to survive. If I hadn't met with you that day they attacked the Raiders, I could be swinging up there with the rest of them."

A shudder runs down Billy's body. Then his mood passes.

"Listen to me croakin' on," he says with a weak smile. "It's done now." He looks up at the dark clouds gathering to the west. "Looks like rain. Let's you and me go and make up some cornmeal biscuits afore we get washed out."

He turns and strides up the hill, leaving me to think that he has human emotions after all.

SEPTEMBER
1864

THIRTEEN 👉

Billy and I learn a lot very quickly in Andersonville. I know Billy said he would teach me the rules, but those were the Raider rules. What we learn after the hangings are prisoner rules, how to survive on your own when people aren't scared of you.

First, never drink anything other than rainwater or water that's been boiled. The water in the swamp is poison. More than a sip or two and you're more than likely to die screaming as your guts turn inside out over the latrines. Diarrhea probably kills more men here than anything else. Fortunately, it rains a lot.

Second, it's impossible to survive on the rations that Wirz gives us. A piece of corn bread the size of a half brick and the occasional small piece of salt pork is not enough to keep a man alive. It will for a while, but then gums begin to bleed, teeth fall out, old scars open up and scurvy takes hold.

Third, burn every scrap you can beg, steal or barter to make a fire as often as possible. This is not only to boil water and dry out occasionally from the eternal rain, but also to kill as many lice as possible. It's futile, you can never get them all, but men who don't kill as many as they can are more likely to get the shivering fever, and that's a death warrant.

Fourth, do everything you can to get a chore outside the stockade. That gives you a chance to barter with the guards or collect a scrap of wood.

Dozens are dying every day, too many even for the dead carts. The bodies are simply dragged or carried down to the gate and dumped, naked, of course— clothes are too valuable to leave on the dead. What is important is to tie a note onto a toe with the man's name scratched on it. That way, he will at least have a tombstone.

Billy and I have quite a thriving business taking bodies down to the gate. Few want to use precious energy dragging a body all the way across the compound, so they are happy enough to let us have the corpse's rags in return for placing a note on the toe and removing the body.

The rags are valuable, as almost everyone who has been here over a few weeks is near naked now. Only new arrivals are well-dressed, and they are continually pestered by beggars and men wanting to trade for socks, a shirt or a jacket. Bargaining rarely works; new men don't yet realize how valuable a handful of brass buttons can be.

I'm sitting outside our lean-to, making a sewing needle. It's a sliver of bone that I have been grinding on a stone for three days now. Tomorrow I will start the slow process of drilling a tiny hole in one end.

Best part of a week to make a needle! Back home, it took a few cents and a minute of time to buy a good steel needle at the store in Broadalbin. It occurs to me that in here we are living like our caveman ancestors did thousands of years ago.

It's raining steadily, and every little while I take off my shirt and wring the water out into a large tin beside the lean-to. This is how we collect drinking water. Lice get wrung out too and scoot around on the surface. I'll fish them out before I next drink.

"Come on, Jake, boy. We've got a job." Billy beckons me from down the hill. I carefully place the needle to one side and stand up. It's a painful process; my joints hurt and I feel dizzy from the effort. It's the first sign of scurvy. I need to get some fresh food soon.

"This's a bad'un," Billy says when I join him, "but I got me a plan." He winks at me with one large sunken eye. "And look what I got to trade." Billy holds out his hand. In the palm is a shiny quarter.

"Where did you get that?" I ask in awe. This is the most valuable thing I've seen in weeks.

"Found it down by the swamp," Billy says casually. "Lucky, eh?"

I don't believe Billy, but I don't push it. He won't tell me. The quarter, like the other things Billy shows up with occasionally, is stolen. Maybe someone even died for this. I don't ask because I don't want to know. If Billy doesn't tell me where things come from, then I can pretend his stories about finding them are true. I don't want to feel guilty. I want fresh food.

Partway down the slope, we come to a small lean-to. The body is lying outside. I recognize it. About two weeks ago a squad of cavalrymen came in with a new batch of prisoners. Most were wounded somewhere, but the sergeant was the worst. His right arm had been taken off above the elbow and his chest was cut up quite badly. He'd been to our hospital outside the stockade and they had cleaned him up as best they could, but there are no bandages here, so he was sent into the stockade with his wounds open and raw.

I saw him the first day he arrived, and already the flies were hovering in a black cloud over his wounds. Now he is dead, and his stump and chest are a seething mass of pale gray maggots. As Billy has said, this is a bad one.

I crouch by the body and begin brushing the maggots off.

"Leave them," Billy says.

"Why?"

"You'll see."

A man crawls out of the lean-to. "You gonna take him?"

Billy nods.

"All right then," the man says. "Here's the paper." The man hands over a grubby scrap of paper with a name written on it. Billy takes a piece of thread and ties it to the dead man's toe.

"You take the head end, Jake," Billy says.

I hesitate; the sergeant's a new arrival, so he's not as skinny as some. To lift him I'll have to put my hands under his armpits. One side's okay, but the other's a mess of maggots. Most of the flesh from the stump of the man's arm and the right side of his chest is eaten away. Through the moving mass, I can see the white gleam of exposed bone.

"It's not far to the gate, Jake. And it'll be worth it, you'll see."

I've grown into the habit of not questioning Billy, and in any case, I don't have the energy to argue. I grit my teeth and lift, trying to ignore the maggots that wriggle onto my hands and arms.

Billy grabs the legs and we set off.

"Some say them maggots is good eating if'n you fry them up over the fire," he says cheerfully. "Me, I ain't got quite that hungry yet.

"Now, Jake, when we get to the gate, you push the side with the maggots good and close up to the guard and let me do the talkin'."

At the gate we ignore the pile of bodies and go straight up to the guard. Like all of them now, he's just a kid.

"Got a bad'un, here," Billy says as I move the maggoty corpse close to the boy. He draws back in horror. "Reckon we'd best take him straight out to the buryin' ground. I sure wouldn't want this thing lyin' aside me fer the rest of the day."

Billy pretends to stumble and the sergeant's stump brushes against the guard, leaving a smear of pus and wriggling maggots on his trousers. The kid brushes at them wildly. He looks as if he's about to throw up.

"So, we'll just take him on out then," Billy says.

"Yes," the guard says in a strangled voice. "Open the gate." The small door set in the main gate creaks open, and Billy and I and the dead sergeant slip through.

"Let's get rid of him and get down to business," Billy says as we head over to the graveyard.

This is the third time I've been outside the stockade on some errand, and it's still hard not to just stand and gawp. There's so much open space and trees, and the crude wooden buildings look like mansions. Even the rain seems less heavy out here.

We carry the sergeant past the ramshackle building that is the Rebel's excuse for a hospital. It's hideously overcrowded and has a death rate higher than within the compound. Even so, there is never enough space to take all the sick who line up at the gate every morning. The ones who get refused are probably lucky. Few come out of the hospital alive.

We set the body down beside a long trench. A group of prisoners is busy extending it at one end, while more cover over the bodies lying in the other end.

"Name's on the toe," Billy says to the guard who's leaning on his musket, looking bored. "We're just goin' to pick up some scraps of wood over by yonder stumps."

"You reckon?" the guard says, standing up straighter.

"I reckon," Billy says, producing two brass buttons from his pocket and slipping them into the guard's hand.

The guard nods and resumes his bored vigil.

We wander over to the edge of the trees and pick up what few twigs and chips from the cut stumps that we can. It would be easy enough to slip off into the trees, but what would be the point? We're so weak now that we wouldn't get far, even if we could get away from the hounds Wirz would send after us. His boast is that on Friday night he could give any two prisoners a twenty-four-hour start and still have them back in time for roll call on Monday morning.

I'm beginning to wonder why Billy went to all the trouble of using the dead sergeant to get us out just for the sake of a few scraps of wood, when a guard steps out of the trees. I expect him to order us back to the stockade, but he steps forward and nods to Billy. I notice he's carrying a sack over his shoulder.

"What you got, Yank?" he says.

"I got this, Reb," Billy says, showing the silver quarter in his open palm.

The guard's eyes widened noticeably.

"I reckon we can get some pretty fair victuals fer this," Billy says. "What you got in that sack?"

The man looks around, crouches down and opens the neck of his sack. I almost faint at the sight of such a possible banquet. There are potatoes, sweet potatoes, onions, and bags of beans and flour. My mouth begins to water uncontrollably.

"Well now." Billy flips the coin and places it back in his pocket. The guard never takes his eyes off it. "I reckon we'd be entitled to a whole parcel of this."

The guard doesn't say anything.

"I've al'ays been partial to onions myself," Billy says, "so we'll begin with those four big yellow ones there."

The guard takes the onions out and places them on the ground.

"See anything you take a fancy to, Jake, boy?"

I can't possibly choose. Everything looks so wonderful. I nod dumbly.

"Seems like my partner here's a bit overwhelmed. Well, I'll just have to decide fer us both. Sweet potatoes."

The guard takes out all the sweet potatoes and piles them beside the onion. There's enough to fill a small bucket. "One more thing," he says.

"Better make it that bag of beans then."

They join the pile. The guard begins to close his sack.

"Cabbage," I manage to blurt out. I know I'm getting scurvy and that any fresh food will help, but I remember reading somewhere that the explorer Captain James Cook fed his sailors cabbage and not a one of them ever got scurvy. Both men stare at me.

"Reckon my partner don't think we're done yet," Billy says with a smile. "Add that nice big cabbage."

The guard hesitates. Billy pulls out the quarter and holds it up. The cabbage joins the pile. The guard takes the quarter, examines it closely and puts it in his pocket.

"I'm only doin' this 'cause the South's beat now," he says.

"Pleasure doin' business with you," Billy says, "but the South's al'ays been beat."

"Sherman's in Atlanta now," the man adds.

We both stare at him. Atlanta. Sherman. "That true?" we ask stupidly.

"True as I'm standing here," the man says. "Atlanta fell and there ain't much stoppin' Sherman marching all the way to Savannah and splittin' the South in two if he's a mind to." He lifts the sack and disappears into the trees.

"The boys must be only thirty or forty miles from Macon. They could be here inside a week," Billy speculates.

I feel a surge of happiness. We could be home for Christmas. To celebrate we eat an onion each, right there by the trees. My tears are only partly from the harsh vegetable, the rest are from sheer joy.

We stuff our treasures into our pockets and I hide the cabbage under my shirt as best I can. On the walk back to the stockade, my joints hurt much less than on the way out.

FOURTEEN

I haff ze good news." Wirz is sitting on his horse at roll call the morning after our excursion outside the gates. I'm feeling better than I have in weeks. We made a cabbage and bean soup last night, and no king ever enjoyed a banquet as much as we enjoyed that soup. The sweet potatoes we buried under the floor of the lean-to for later. Our neighbors watch us enviously but fear of Billy's blade keeps them at bay.

"Zere iz to be a parole." A buzz of excited conversation runs through the assembled prisoners. Parole home on a prisoner exchange is our dream, but the story is that General Grant has forbidden it because the Rebels refuse to include black soldiers in any exchange. Maybe he's changed his mind.

"You vill assemble here zis afternoon at vun of ze clock. Ze first batch vill go to Savannah to get ze boats home." Wirz turns his horse and rides out the gate. The buzz of conversation turns into a chorus of ragged cheers. Everyone disperses back to their shelters to prepare.

"We're going home," I say excitedly to Billy as we trek up the hill.

Billy just grunts. I'm annoyed that he doesn't seem to share the general excitement.

"It's great news. If we can get on the first batch, we'll be in Savannah in a few days and home in two weeks. God dammit, Billy, be happy. We've survived."

"I ain't so sure. How do we know Wirz ain't lyin'?"

"Why would he lie?"

"Look at this place, Jake. There's thirty thousand dyin' men packed in here as tight as those bodies in the grave behind the hospital. It's Hell fer sure. Maybe Sherman's on his way here already. Would you want to be caught as the commandant of Hell?"

"No." I wonder where Billy's going with this.

"So, if Wirz ships out ten or twenty thousand of us, those left would look much better."

"Are you suggesting that we stay? That we don't take the parole?" I ask in horror.

"Fer the time bein', yes."

"You're crazy!" I yell. Anger sweeps over me. I can't believe what Billy's saying. "Staying here is committing suicide as surely as stepping over the dead line. Even if Wirz is lying, wherever they take us can't be worse than this."

Billy shrugs. "You make your decision, Jake. I've made mine." He turns away. I grab his arm.

"Why, Billy?"

"Because this place will get better after a few thousand leave. Better the devil you know…"

"That's no reason," I rage. "You choose to stay, hoping that things will get better here, and maybe they will, but there'll still be poisonous water, no food, cruel guards and a pile of bodies at the gate every morning."

"And what if Sherman is on his way here?" Billy interrupts. "You walk out that gate, get on a train and in two weeks time your sittin' in a camp just as bad as this outside Savannah awaitin' ships that ain't never gonna come 'cause Wirz was lyin'. Meanwhile, I'm sleepin' 'tween fresh sheets in Atlanta with a couple of pretty nurses tendin' to my every need."

Billy attempts a smile, but it has no effect on me. I shake him to try and get him to see sense.

"I've been here almost three months," I say. "Hasn't been a day or a night that I haven't dreamt of walking out that gate and never looking back. Here's our chance."

"I know what you mean, Jake. I have the same thoughts."

"Then why stay?"

Billy looks thoughtful for a minute. "Say it is a parole," he says, eventually. "What'll you do?"

"What'll I do? I'll have a bath, put on new clothes, eat the biggest meal you've ever seen—"

"No. I mean after all that."

"I'll go home. Soon as I'm strong enough, I'll let Ma fuss over me and Pa be proud. I'll get my horse and ride around the farm, maybe go into town and just sit in the sun telling stories. And I'll go fishing. There's a big fish I promised someone I'd catch."

Billy nods. "Home," he repeats wistfully. "See, that's where you and me is different. I ain't never had one of them."

"Everybody has a home."

"Not me. My daddy drank hisself to death afore I can really remember him, and Ma took in 'friends' to buy food for me and my sisters. We moved around a lot, al'ays tryin' to find someplace cheaper to live and stay one step ahead of the cops. Ain't no place I got a yearnin' to return to."

Billy lets out a dry laugh.

"What's so funny?" I ask.

"Well, all your talk of home. If I have to pick someplace that means somethin' to me, it'd have to be here." Billy swings his arm in a wide arc to take in the stockade.

"Andersonville?"

"I ain't sayin' it's paradise. Nothin' like the home you're lookin' forward to, with home-baked apple pies and fishin' and such, but I'm somebody in here. When I was a Raider, folks respected me. I know it was 'cause they feared the blade and such, but respect's respect, and I ain't never had that afore. Ain't never likely to again, I daresay.

"Now, I ain't a Raider no more, but the blade can still get me some respect when I need it. And I'm survivin'. We're survivin'. Survivin' when a whole lot of folk ain't. I'm good at survivin', Jake. Ain't never been good at nothin' my whole life and, once I'm out of here, I daresay I won't be good at nothin' again, least nothin' that will keep me out of prison or not lead me to a back alley with my throat slit. This is all the home I got, Jake. I'll be stayin'."

I look hard at Billy. How can anyone think this hell is home? I try to imagine what a life that can make Andersonville look good must have been like. I fail.

"But we're a team, Billy. You always said that. We've got to stick together."

"So stay with me, Jake. I ain't askin' you to think on this place as home, but don't trust Wirz. This parole thing's too easy. Life ain't like that."

"I don't know."

"So think on it. Ain't no way Wirz'll get all those he wants out today or even listed. Just hang back a little is all I'm sayin'."

"Okay," I say reluctantly. "I won't rush to be at the head of the queue, but I'll not miss my chance."

"Fair enough," Billy says with a smile. "Now, let's see what we can get from them boys that's keen to be the first to leave."

The pickings are good as we wander round the hillside. Many soldiers are eager to barter anything they cannot carry with them. We pick up a good tarpaulin for our lean-to and some solid sticks that we can either use as supports or burn.

Billy is happy. "See, we can live like kings once these boys is gone. And the pickin's is only gonna get better."

I'm not so sure. In the short term we'll be more comfortable because of what we've acquired this morning, but not comfortable enough to make me want to stay. But I'm confused. Billy has made what should have been simple—get on the train to Savannah and go home—complicated. What if it's a cruel trick? And there's more to it than that.

The home that I yearn for is a dream. When I sit and picture what going home will be like, everything is perfect—it never rains, every meal is sumptuous, Ma and Pa are always smiling. Sometimes I even imagine myself catching the big trout, and at those times it's hard not to imagine Jim there beside me. I know it won't be like that. Jim is dead and I have no idea how Ma and Pa are coping with the war, Jim's death and my absence.

On top of all that, there's what I'll be carrying home with me. Nathaniel still stares at me accusingly in my dreams, and I carry around my neck the weight of all the things I suspect Billy has done to help keep us alive. While I'm in here, I can rationalize what we do to stay alive, but in the real world, where people don't kill and cheat and steal to survive, how will I handle all of that?

What do I say when Ma makes me a perfect supper, ruffles my hair and asks, "What was it like in Andersonville?"

"Well, Ma, my best friend was a thief and a killer, and I held a kid while he stabbed him to death."

It'll all have to stay inside, and how hard will that be?

"Jake, can you do me a favor?" I look up to see who's spoken. It's Sam from the Raiders, who was with us when we killed Nathaniel and who was beaten running the gauntlet. He lives in a nearby lean-to and sometimes comes over to talk about old times. I remember him as a brutal, foul-mouthed man, but the beating and the starvation have mellowed him. Now he seems almost apologetic all the time and pitifully grateful for any favor we do for him.

"Can you help me," he says when he sees me look at him.

I grunt and go over to where he's sitting in the mud. Physically, he's not in too bad shape, although he's been complaining about his feet recently. Like everyone else, he's almost delirious at the thought of parole.

"We're going home, Jake," he says with a broad grin.

"I reckon," I say non-committally.

"But I got a problem, Jake." Sam pulls aside the blanket that's covering his feet and I recoil in horror.

"They ain't pretty, are they?"

Almost all the flesh from his toes has rotted away, except for a small pad at the end of each. I can see the bones and the ligaments that are holding everything in place.

Sam holds up a pair of dull, rusty shears. "Can you cut my toes off?"

"No," I say instinctively. "Go to the hospital and have one of the doctors do it."

Sam shakes his head. "You know the chances of coming out of that place is slim, and I don't want no Rebel butcher messing up my feet. Besides, there ain't time if we're to be leaving this afternoon. I can't walk like this. The toes don't hurt much no more, but if I try and walk, I trip on them and then my whole foot pains me like the devil."

"I can't," I say helplessly.

"Oh, come on, Jake," Sam whines. "They're my toes and I want them off. Take the shears and cut them. You wouldn't deny me the chance to go home, would you?"

I take a deep breath and grasp the shears he's holding out. The snipping is remarkably quick, although some of the tendons are tough. There's no blood and my operation doesn't seem to hurt. In a minute there's a pile of toe bones on the ground.

"That's better," Sam says. "Daresay I'll have trouble with balance for a day or two, but I won't care about that when I'm home, and I won't never have to worry about corns. Thank you very kindly, Jake."

I nod acknowledgment and return to the lean-to with another burden of memory that I'll never be able to share with anyone outside this place.

SEPTEMBER 1864
TO
APRIL 1865

FIFTEEN

Long before one o'clock, everyone is collected by the main gate. Most are carrying their pitiful belongings wrapped in whatever they have that passes for a blanket. The assumption seems to be that the gates will just be flung open and we will all just stagger out and go home. After what seems like an interminable wait, the gates creak open. Like a single creature, the crowd tenses and leans forward. But it's only Wirz on his pale horse.

"I zee you are ready to go home," he begins. Something like a moan runs through the crowd. "Vell, ze ships are vaiting in Savannah. I tell you how it vill be. Detachments vun through tventy, zat is tventy thousand men, vill be exchanged. Ze trains for detachments vun though five wait now at the ze station zis afternoon. Ze rest tomorrow. Farevell."

That's it. Wirz turns his horse and rides out the gate, leaving twenty thousand happy and a few thousand despondent prisoners. I don't know which to be. My choice has been made for me. Billy and I are to stay.

"I told you Wirz was lyin'," Billy says cheerfully.

"What do you mean?"

"He just wants to clear out the camp, make it respectable lookin' fer Sherman comin'. Do you really think there's a Union fleet big enough to take twenty thousand men sittin' in the Savannah docks?"

"I suppose not." I'm uncertain though. Detachments one through five are already filing out the gate, and the rest of the compound is a hubbub of conversation. Those chosen to stay are busy writing letters to family and persuading those about to leave to take them with them. Those leaving are loudly swearing that they won't rest until everyone else is exchanged as well.

"Come on, Jake. We got work to do if we want to live like kings until Sherman gets here."

Billy and I increase our store of sticks and tent material through bartering with the men leaving. We even move up to an open area higher up the hill and take over a bigger, more secure shelter. It's dug into the ground about two feet, which helps keep it warm. Two sleeping benches are formed a few inches off the ground, and a ditch to carry away any water that collects in the bottom, helps keep us dry.

———•———

A week after Wirz's announcement, there are only about six thousand men left in Andersonville. Few apart from Billy are happy to be left behind, but conditions improve dramatically almost immediately. There is enough stuff left lying around for everyone to improve their shelter significantly, and it's now possible to walk across the compound in more or less a straight line without wending a tortuous way between closely packed tents and lean-tos. The air suddenly seems cleaner and even the creek shows signs of improving, although anyone with any sense still drinks only rainwater.

The food doesn't improve in either quality or quantity, but the guards seem more relaxed and bartering for luxuries becomes easier.

But Billy is wrong in thinking that Sherman is coming to free us. As winter drags on, we wait, but one day is like the next. New prisoners brought in say they heard that a sergeant from Andersonville escaped to Sherman's camp and pleaded for an expedition to free the prisoners before they all starved.

Story is that Sherman refused because thirty thousand mouths to feed and bodies to guard was a significant drain on the stretched resources of the Confederacy and would hasten its collapse. Can a man be so cold-hearted as to let such suffering as we see here go on if it is within his power to stop it? I don't know. Perhaps it's just a story. But if it's true, would it be any worse than General Grant sending us against the Rebel breastworks and guns at Cold Harbor with our names pinned to our backs?

It's better with only five or six thousand of us in the stockade, but even the starvation rations are cut and the guards have less and less to trade. In fact, some of them look almost as starved as we do.

The days are the same—a hopeless, energy-sapping search for food, firewood and shelter. Through all the bleak winter months it rains endlessly. The only thing that changes is that we gradually get weaker and lose interest in everything. When I can be bothered, I wander around looking for scraps of wood or something I can trade for food. I have to sit and rest a lot. Sometimes, in the middle of the camp, I am completely overcome by an inexplicable, gut-wrenching sadness. I have to sit down and weep until it passes. At other times, something random, the way a starving man's cheekbones stick out of his face or the green color of another's gangrenous foot, will strike me as the funniest thing I have ever seen and I will laugh until I cry. I think I might be going crazy.

Billy is not much better. I think he might be going crazy too, but his madness has a mean streak. I have to be careful what I say so that he doesn't take offence. More than once he's threatened me with his blade. At other times he is almost frighteningly optimistic, swearing that he can hear Sherman's cavalry riding toward us, or devising complex schemes for escape.

"The trick is to stick to the rivers," he says one day as we sit lethargically outside our shelter on one of the few days when the rain holds off. "Wirz ain't right when he says he can give any two men a twenty-four-hour head start and still catch them. Twenty-four hours is plenty time to make it to the river. Ain't no hound born as can follow a man if'n he sticks to water, and I'll wager you could go all the way to Atlanta without puttin' more'n a foot out of a river or creek."

"Let's ask Wirz if he'll give us a start," I suggest. Suddenly, the idea seems so funny that I burst out laughing.

"What?" Billy asks.

"There's one problem with your plan," I say between sobbing laughs.

"What's that?" Billy asks indignantly.

"Wirz can give us all the start we want, it won't matter. We haven't the strength to reach the river in the first place."

Billy looks angry; then he starts laughing too. "Reckon you'd be right there, Jake, boy. We're a sorry pair and no mistake. But we're alive and that's worth somethin'. Ain't too many here can say that. Must be twelve, thirteen thousand boys buried out in that cemetery yonder."

I sigh and use my tongue to probe the hole where one of my teeth fell out three days before. A pair of swallows zoom no more than a couple of feet over our heads, bank sharply and disappear over the stockade wall. "But we can't last forever, and sometimes that's how long I think this war's going to last."

"Naw," Billy says. "Can't be much longer. South must be just about done. New prisoners comin' in is gettin' fewer and fewer. That's a sign that the Rebs ain't winnin' too many battles no more, and when new boys do come in, they got tales of victory. Why, that squad come in last month, the ones brung us the biscuits, they said Sherman took Savannah way back at Christmas and ole Lee's bottled up at Petersburg. We ain't gonna be here much longer."

"That's what you said back in September when Sherman took Atlanta, and here we are still."

Billy's sunken eyes flash with anger. "Well, if'n you want to sit and feel sorry fer yourself, you go right ahead, Jake. Me, I prefer to look at the positives and I reckon' we'll be out of here afore you know it."

Billy gets laboriously to his feet and stretches. A swallow narrowly misses his head. "Damn those birds," he says, shaking his fist at the air. Then he stops and stares out over the camp. Swallows are darting low over the whole scene.

"What d'you reckon them birds is doin'?" he asks.

"Feeding," I say. "Must be a good crop of fat bugs rising up off our sorry carcasses. Enough to keep a swallow or two happy, I should think."

"We still got that piece of nettin' them sailors brung in back in January?"

"Yeah," I say. "We use it to keep our food off the ground and away from the rats. Or we would if we had any food anymore."

"Bring it out," Billy says. "I'm gonna find me a couple of nice rocks."

In a daze, I do as I'm told. The net's torn in several places and ragged along one edge, but I've never seen the need to mend it. It can't keep you warm and there are no fish here.

Billy returns with two medium-sized stones. With some difficulty, he ties them onto two corners of the netting.

"Watch this, Jake, boy," he says and stands looking out over the camp. Two swallows dart over toward us and Billy hurls the stones up. He mistimes his throw and misses by a fair bit, but I get the idea.

"Give me one of the rocks," I say.

We miss twelve times, but on the thirteenth, a swallow becomes entangled in the net and Billy whoops with glee as it falls to the ground. He grabs the panicking bird and wrings its neck.

"We're gonna have soup tonight," he says. "Help me catch another couple."

We're so engrossed in our new sport that we don't hear the message being shouted over the camp. We've just caught our third bird when I hear a voice shout, "Richmond!"

"I wish we had some vegetable to go with these," Billy muses as he wrings the bird's neck. "Remember those sweet potatoes we got fer that quarter. I wish…"

"Shut up," I say harshly. "Listen."

"Richmond's fallen!" The word is spreading across the camp like wildfire. Figures are dragging themselves out of shelters all over and staggering upright.

"Richmond's fallen!" A ragged cheer echoes over the camp. Someone starts singing "The Battle Cry of Freedom." Someone else begins "The Girl I Left Behind Me."

"Richmond's fallen!" I slump down, suddenly exhausted. Can it be true or is it another vicious trick?

"I told you, Jake, boy," Billy says. "We're goin' home soon."

APRIL 1865

SIXTEEN 👉

Ain't no guards!"

The cry wakes me from a fitful sleep and dreams of Nathaniel and food. I have no idea what it means, but whatever it is, it's not worth expending the energy required to crawl out of the shelter.

What day is it? I begin my morning ritual of working out the day and how long I have been in here. It is the only way I can convince myself that each day is not the same as yesterday and that time is actually passing.

It's April 9. No. That was yesterday. It must be April 10 today. April 10, 1865. Now for the hard bit.

"They're gone. Every one of them."

What's going on outside? I wish everyone would shut up, so I can work out how long I've been here. It's hard enough to focus without all this shouting.

It's April 10, 1865, and I arrived here on June 28, 1864. That's eight, no, nine months to March 28. And how many days? Ten in April now and the three after March 28. That makes thirteen. Nine months and thirteen days in Hell.

I feel ridiculously happy that I have worked it out again, that I am still alive to work it out.

It's three days since the news was passed around that Richmond had fallen. That night was like a huge party in the camp. We sang every song anybody knew, and those that could danced while the guards watched us sullenly from their towers.

Billy and I feasted on swallow soup. We threw them into the pot and ate them, skin, guts and all. It was a feast all right. Trouble was that it gave me the runs so bad I was at the latrine all next day with the cramps. Since then, all I've eaten is a rotten corncob.

"They truly are gone." Billy rips the tent door open.

"Who's gone?" I ask.

"The guards. Ain't a one of them left on the stockade. You got to come and see."

I want to ignore Billy, but he grabs my arm and

hauls me through the tent door. I struggle to my feet and look around.

Those of the five thousand men left in the camp who can walk or crawl are headed toward the gate, where a sizeable crowd is forming.

"Come on," Billy says, tugging my arm. "Let's go see what's goin' on."

I don't want to. I just want to lie down, but Billy insists.

The crowd is standing at the dead line, staring at the gate and chattering.

"Is the gate locked?"

"Where are the guards?"

"What should we do?"

It's Billy that decides.

"Ain't gonna live forever," he says and ducks under the line.

The crowd instantly falls silent. Billy takes a step forward and stops. Nothing happens. He takes another step. The crowd is looking at the stockade and empty watchtowers nervously.

"Hey, Johnny Reb," Billy shouts. "You gonna shoot me?"

No one answers. I can't even hear anyone breathing. The silence is almost solid.

Billy walks slowly forward until he's at the gate. He grabs the iron bar nailed to one side and hauls. With a groan that makes everyone jump, the gate swings in.

Still, nobody crosses the dead line. Some adjust their position so they can see out through the widening gap as Billy pulls the gate open.

"Come on," Billy shouts, turning back to us. "Ain't no one here. You want to stay in this place forever?"

Someone pulls down the sticks that mark the dead line. We all shuffle forward and stare with disbelief at the world outside. There's grass and trees and birds. Are we free?

In slow motion, the crowd spills out the gate. Stunned skeletal figures wander aimlessly off in all directions, unable to understand their freedom.

A burst of noise at one corner of the stockade makes everyone turn in fear. Five men on horses canter into view. They look so clean, fit and well-fed compared to the staggering corpses outside the gate. They look like gods. Only one of their horses would feed us all for a whole day.

I'm so overwhelmed that it takes a minute to realize that they are dressed in Union blue. The officer at the front canters forward and stops in the middle of the group. His face is a mask of horror.

"My God," he whispers. "What place is this?"

I take a stumbling step forward and croak out an answer. "Andersonville. I've been here for nine months and thirteen days." I don't know why I tell him that. It seems important.

A vague thought sluggishly forces its way into my brain. This man is from the outside world. He probably knows what's happening.

"How's the war going?" I ask.

"War's over," the officer says with a smile. "Lee surrendered to General Grant yesterday at Appomattox Court House. What happened here?"

A thin smile forms on my face as I answer. "We survived."

SEVENTEEN

ever thought army biscuits could taste so good." Billy and I are sitting in the spring sun on the grassy slope above the stockade. All around, men are sitting or walking about. Some just stand and stare, still stunned by their freedom. Others are still in the stockade, too sick to move.

The cavalrymen who arrived this morning gave us all the rations they had. Fortunately, it wasn't much, just some biscuits and dried meat. We would have eaten anything they gave us, and the doctor who arrived in the middle of the day said that too much rich food too suddenly could kill us in our weakened state. It would be cruel to die of too much food now that we are free.

Free. I still can hardly believe it. I can do what I want. Or, I could if I was strong enough. What do I want? I want to get my strength back and leave the war behind and go home. Most of all, I want to forget.

"We made it," Billy says.

"We did that," I agree. I'm happy that I survived, except for one thing.

Seems like every night I still see Nathaniel's ghost. As soon as I close my eyes, he comes to me and just stands there, looking all pitiful and surprised, with Billy's knife sticking out of his chest. He never says anything, but I know what he's asking. Why? Why is he dead and I'm alive? Why didn't I protect him?

I have no answers. In the daylight I can rationalize that Nathaniel was doomed from the start. He would never have lasted in Hell for long and all Billy's knife did was shorten his suffering. But nothing I think of stops the nighttime visits from his poor, sad corpse. I'm haunted. I can go home now, but I fear I'll take a part of Hell with me.

"A lot didn't make it," I say, thinking of Nathaniel but looking at the cemetery where the rough crosses mark the long mass graves.

"Remember the day they hanged Mosby twice?" Billy asks with a smile.

I nod.

"Them five other Raiders swinging there, kicking air, and Mosby in a pile on the ground, cursing and rubbing his neck." We both laugh at the memory.

"Mosby's mistake was that he got too big," I say. "Thought he could control the whole camp. Your idea to keep a low profile and not upset too many people was much better."

"It was too, and we managed that pretty well, didn't we, Jake?"

"We did," I say.

We sit in a nostalgic silence. But gradually the cost of us living well worms its way into my mind. I've always tried to ignore the things Billy has done to help us survive, but I'm sure some of the crosses on the hillside are there because of Billy, and me. The old crazy man when we got our first shelter after the Raiders were defeated, whoever owned that shiny quarter that bought us the vegetables the day the parole was announced. And how many others died because they lacked that blanket or piece of food that Billy stole? Billy did the killing, but those deaths are on my head just as surely as if I had wielded the knife myself. I tell myself that we did what we had to do to survive, we had no choice, but is there a price that's too high to pay, even for survival?

"For a while we lived pretty good," Billy says almost wistfully.

"We did," I agree, "but do you reckon it was worth what we did?"

"What do you mean?" Billy asks. "'Course it was worth it. We're alive, ain't we? Surviving, that's what's important. You said as much yourself."

"I know. Don't listen to me. I'm just moaning." Suddenly I'm too tired to talk about the cost anymore. I just want to get home and forget. We lapse into silence.

"What d'you reckon'll happen next?" Billy asks eventually.

"Well, the war's over and we're not prisoners anymore, but we're still soldiers. I reckon they'll feed us up a bit, take us down to either Savannah or Vicksburg, discharge us and put us on a ship up the coast or a riverboat up the Mississippi."

Billy nods. "I like the feeding idea. And the riverboat. Ain't never bin on one of them. Then what?"

"Home," I say.

Billy falls silent. I immediately regret mentioning home after what he told me about Andersonville being the only home he's ever had. I want to say something, reassure him, but what can I say? Over the months, Billy and I have become close. We've helped each other out and each of us is probably the main reason the other is still alive, but we are very different. I trust Billy more now, but that is only because his fate is tied to mine. And because we both know about the things we've done to survive that we would rather no one else knew about.

I suppose the main difference between Billy and me is that I feel sorry for the poor soldiers we robbed, although that didn't make me stop stealing or prevent Billy. I lay awake at night; Billy slept like a baby. No nightmares about sticking his knife under Nathaniel's ribs kept him awake.

Does feeling badly about what we have done to survive make me a better person than Billy? I don't know.

I lie back on the grass and close my eyes. The sun is warm on my face. Soon, Billy and I will go our separate ways and I can begin to forget.

EIGHTEEN

ook at this, boys. Sherman sure didn't leave much of Atlanta for those Rebs."

We crowd the train carriage windows and look out on the blackened ruins of the city that General Sherman burned before he set off on his march to Savannah and the sea. Stone chimneys, cracked walls and churches are about all that still stand above the rubble. Roads have been cleared and new tracks have been laid for the train. There are soldiers, cavalry and military wagons everywhere. It's the morning of April 16, and we're on our way home.

"Serves them right," Billy says. "They started this damned war." Grunts of agreement pass around the carriage. "Where do we go from here?"

"If we go east, it's Savannah. If we go west, it's Vicksburg."

We all look out the windows at the devastation as the train crawls along. Gradually we swing around until we are heading away from the morning sun.

"Looks like Vicksburg," I say to Billy. "You'll get your chance to go on a riverboat."

We slow to a walking pace as we pass a Union camp. Tents stretch as far as the eye can see, and huge piles of supplies, ammunition and guns are everywhere.

I still haven't got used to how healthy everyone looks compared to us or the Andersonville guards.

"How did the South think they could beat us?" I ask to no one in particular as we gaze at the wealth and power spread out before us.

But something's wrong. Soldiers are standing around in small groups, talking instead of going about their chores. There's a sense of agitation over everything.

"Ain't right." Billy's noticed it too. He pulls a window down and leans out.

"What's goin' on?" he asks the closest group of men.

"Lincoln's been shot," one of the men shouts back. "Just come over the telegraph."

"Shot?" Billy asks.

"Shot dead," the man replies. "At a play up in Washington, night afore last."

The men in the carriage are silent. This is a shock. Lincoln was the symbol of the Union.

"Who done it?" a man at the back of the carriage shouts.

Billy passes on the question, but we're too far away to hear the answer.

"Some Southerner, I reckon," someone else says.

The rest of the journey is spent in alternating spells of thoughtful silence and wild speculation. Lincoln has become a symbol of the Union and, now, of our victory. Does his death mean that the South will rise up again? Probably not, they are too well beaten, but it's not my concern. I want to go home and not ever think about politics or war again.

At dusk we arrive at a large camp outside Vicksburg. As we get down from the train, I notice that the flags in front of the officer's quarters are flying at half-mast. We are divided into squads and assigned tents.

The place is called Camp Fisk, and the inhabitants are from prison camps all over the South. All have the gaunt, starved look of those of us from Andersonville, but there's a world of difference. Here everyone has a good tent, new clothes, and plenty of firewood and food. There's even a large clean hospital tent without mass graves behind it.

Billy and I are sitting by a roaring fire outside our tent with full bellies and sipping on the first coffee we have tasted in months. I can hardly believe how many fires there are around the camp and how big they all are. At Andersonville we fought for and treasured sticks the thickness of a finger. Here anyone can casually throw a log as thick as a leg on and watch it burn in a few minutes.

"Jake. Billy." I look up to see a figure coming toward us through the flickering light. He's walking strangely, stiff-legged and with small steps.

"I seen you come in this evening," the stranger says. "Thought I'd give you a chance to settle afore I come over and say howdy."

I stare at the man. He looks vaguely familiar, but I can't place him. He's well-fed and clean shaven.

"You boys don't recognize me." The man laughs. "It's Sam from the Raiders."

"Sam!" Billy jumps to his feet. "How in the hell are you?"

"I can't complain, Billy."

"You can walk," I say, looking at his feet with a shudder.

"Sure can," Sam says. "It took a while to learn to balance after I left them toes back in Andersonville, but I'm mighty obliged to you, Jake. I'd be dead for sure if you hadn't helped me out."

"Sit down," Billy says. "Have a cup of coffee. It ain't as good as some I can remember, but it's better than swamp water."

We sit and reminisce.

"You were right about the parole," Sam says. "Wirz was lying through his teeth, as usual. We were taken to Savannah as promised, but there were no ships waiting for us. We were moved around quite a bit, especially when Sherman began his march to the sea. Eventually, they moved us to a stockade at a place called Florence. It was a small copy of Andersonville, but at least we had clean water and the guards weren't too cruel, though it seemed like every week there was less food and men were dying regular of scurvy and the fever. I was lucky. Because of my feet, I got a job as orderly to the camp commander. I managed to sneak a bit of extra food and got to sleep out of the rain in the back of the store shed."

I think that, judging from Sam's plump cheeks, he has managed to sneak a lot of extra food.

"We kept hearing stories from new prisoners and slaves about how the Confederacy was going to hell.

At the beginning of March, we were loaded onto a train and taken to Wilmington, where we were handed over to our own boys.

"Those were good days," Sam says wistfully. "Seems like we had roast chicken and potatoes for near every meal. Then they shipped us over here."

"How long have you been here?" I ask.

Sam concentrated for a minute. "Near enough to six weeks, I reckon."

"Six weeks!" Billy sounds horrified. "I ain't stayin' here fer six weeks. Where are the riverboats?"

"They're in Vicksburg all right, and a lot of the boys have gone home, but they don't run the boats special for us. Whatever's coming north on the river is loaded up."

"How do you get on one?" Billy asks.

"Well," Sam says, "system is the riverboat captains get paid five government dollars a head for every man they take north."

"That's good money," Billy comments.

"Sure is, but the captains don't get it all. Major Heath—he's in charge of the shipments—gets his cut. And, you might say, the Major's open to persuasion. It's no coincidence that the folks with a little something stashed away were on the first boats. Now, those of us left got nothing to persuade with, so Heath ain't in a hurry. I think he and the quartermaster got a deal to skim off the rations for this place and sell it to any Southerners with any valuables left."

"That's ridiculous," I say indignantly. "For months we were beaten and mistreated by the enemy and now the same thing's happening with men on our side."

Sam shrugged. "Won't be more than a few days now anyway. Can't be more than a few thousand of us left here, and the river's busy now that spring's arrived. Just sit back and get your strength back."

NINETEEN

I'm doing exactly what Sam suggested, but it's harsh being stuck in limbo. Men are beginning to waste what energy they have on pointless arguments, and fights break out somewhere in the camp every day.

It's been a week and there's still as many men here at Fisk as when Billy and I arrived. We've watched trainloads of men arrive, be processed and be on a riverboat in two or three days while we stay and rot. We're not rotting physically like some did in Andersonville. There's two meals a day, toilets you can barely smell and no stockade wall to stop you taking a stroll if you have the strength and the spirit moves you. Billy's taken to excusing himself from camp for long periods of time. It's not strictly allowed, but no one cares too much. Last night, Billy didn't return to camp at all and I had to cover for him at roll call. I assume he's out enjoying the pleasures of Vicksburg.

"Come on, Jake, let's go."

"Where?" I look up to see Billy and Sam standing over me. Billy's carrying a small sack in his left hand.

"Vicksburg, of course. Sam and me, we're gettin' us out of this place."

Billy looks almost human again and his old cockiness is back. He is still skinny but, like all of us, he has benefited mightily from his time here. The weakest and sickest have died or are in hospitals in town, so the two thousand or so of us left here are relatively fit and eager to move on.

I suppose my mother would be shocked if she could see me now, but I am a different person from a month ago. I'm still weak and have trouble walking any great distance, but I have enough flesh on my bones not to rub my joints raw on my coarse uniform as I move.

"How do you plan to get us out?"

"I ain't been sittin' around wastin' my time. I been in town workin'." Billy smiles slyly. "There's a big riverboat at the dock, big enough to take at least half the men here up the river to Cairo. I bin talkin' to the captain."

"Why does he listen to you?" I ask. "You're not even an officer."

Billy winks broadly. "I got my ways, Jake, boy. Now, come on. I got us a ride into town on a supply wagon, and we got to see Major Heath afore it leaves."

Billy leads the way through camp toward the supply shed. Sam and I follow behind, me wondering what business Billy has cooked up with Heath, and Sam moving as best he can with his awkward gait. There's an officer standing outside the door, supervising some soldiers offloading flour sacks from a wagon. Billy approaches the officer and salutes smartly.

"Beggin' your pardon, Major Heath, sir," Billy says. "I got those items we was discussin'."

Heath looks at us like we're something unpleasant he's just stepped on. "Who are these?"

"My partners, sir," Billy says. "I can vouch fer them, sir. Good lads, both."

"Very well. Come on." Heath leads us round the side of the building. I instinctively don't like the man. He has the same arrogant superiority that Wirz had, and I feel he would get rid of anyone who got in his way without losing a moment's sleep.

"Let's see then," Heath says when we are out of sight.

Billy unties the neck of the bag and tips the contents out onto the ground. We all crouch down to look.

It's a collection of valuables—silver coins, some grubby banknotes, two pocket watches and, glittering on the top of the pile, a diamond necklace.

Heath picks up the necklace and examines it closely. "Nice," he says. "Where'd you say you got this stuff?"

"Donations from the boys in camp that wants a place on the riverboat."

"And one of them boys just happened to have a diamond necklace in his pocket?"

Billy shrugs and Sam grins.

"Well, no matter." Heath scoops the valuables back into the bag and stands. "I'll not ask too many questions. You and your partners and whoever else you *persuaded* to part with their valuables have places on the riverboat. Go and see Mason and tell him the trains will be coming this afternoon and to be ready to sail tonight with a full load. I'll follow you into town."

Heath strides off toward the officer's quarters. Sam and I follow Billy back to the now empty supply wagon and climb onto the back.

It's four miles into Vicksburg along a bumpy wagon road, but I don't notice the discomfort. I'm preoccupied with thoughts of where Billy got that bag of valuables.

I can easily imagine him and Sam going round the camp collecting money and the watches in exchange for a place on the riverboat, although I'm surprised at the quality of the pickings. What I don't understand is where the necklace came from. That's not the sort of keepsake a soldier would carry.

"Who'd you get the necklace from?" I ask.

"You'd be surprised what some folks carry," Billy responds. He and Sam laugh.

"It looked valuable."

"Don't you worry, Jake. I ain't fool enough to give Heath everythin' I got. There's plenty more stashed away fer a rainy day."

"It just doesn't seem like something you could get from a soldier."

Billy stares hard at me. "We ain't in Andersonville no more. The rules is different in the real world. Now, let's just say I come upon that necklace and saw the chance to dazzle Heath with it.

"Besides, Jake, boy"—Billy smiles at me—"that necklace is payin' fer your place on that riverboat. It's your ticket home, and ain't that where you want to go?"

I nod and we ride the rest of the way in silence. Nothing has changed. Billy, now with Sam in tow, is up to his old ways, and I am benefiting from it. I have two choices: challenge Billy and stay in Camp Fisk, or push my suspicions to the back of my mind and start the journey home tonight. As usual, I keep silent.

TWENTY

The Mississippi is swollen with spring runoff and rolls past in a powerful brown surge on its way to New Orleans. River traffic is heavy in both directions, and the docks are full of all kinds of craft loading and unloading. Billy leads us straight to the largest vessel I have ever seen.

The riverboat is 260 feet long and her four decks rise to the height of a tall building. Two black smokestacks tower above that, and her huge side paddle wheels carry her name in letters taller than a man—*Sultana*. The red of her hull and the white of her decking are faded and rust-spotted from hard wartime service on the river, but she's still a magnificent sight.

"Don't gawk, Jake." Billy slaps me on the shoulder. "Your jaw's hanging open like a country bumpkin on his first visit to the city."

"She's beautiful," I stammer.

"Ain't she just. Built in St. Louis but two years ago. She's the pride of the river."

"What are those men doing?" I notice gangs of workmen hammering beams into place between the decks.

"Reinforcing her decks," Billy explains. "The *Sultana*'s goin' to be carryin' a lot of our boys home."

I want to ask Billy why the decks need to be reinforced on such a new vessel, but I don't get the chance. Billy and Sam are heading over to the gangway, where a well-dressed short man with a neatly trimmed chin beard is standing.

"Who's this?" The man asks, staring at me with two of the most piercing blue eyes I have ever seen.

"This is my partner, Jake Clay," Billy says with a smile. "Jake, meet Captain J. Cass Mason, the man who holds the steamboat record for the fastest trip from New Orleans to St. Louis."

Mason relaxes at the compliment. "Where's Heath?" he asks.

"He'll be here," Billy reassures him.

"Cap'n Mason." An oil-stained sailor jogs down the gangway. "Engineer says that crack in boiler number three needs cutting out and a new patch welded in."

Mason turns to the man. "How long does he say it'll take?"

"Two, maybe three days." The man shrugs.

"We can't wait that long," Billy interrupts.

Mason looks uncertain.

"You want to see them soldiers board other boats?" Billy asks, waving his arms at the smaller steamboats lined along the docks.

Mason takes a deep breath. "Tell him to weld a patch over the crack."

"It won't be as strong," the man says.

"Then we'll repair it proper when we get up to St. Louis," Mason snaps. "Now go tell the engineer to fix it and be quick."

"Is it safe?" I ask as the man returns to the *Sultana*.

"'Course it is," Billy says confidently. "The patch'll hold easy to St. Louis. Right, Cap'n Mason?"

Mason nods, but he looks worried. "Here's Heath," he says, looking over my shoulder.

Billy, Sam and I salute as Heath, in a clean perfectly pressed uniform, strides up.

Heath nods a curt acknowledgment.

"Now, Mason." Heath turns to the captain. "How many men can the *Sultana* take?"

"Well, sir, we've got seventy-three paying passengers, eighty-five crew and the *Sultana*'s rated to carry 376. So—"

"Three hundred and seventy six!" Heath shouts. "With your damned passengers and crew," he hesitates a moment, calculating, "that only leaves 218 spaces. What in hell's going on, Sharp? Two hundred's barely worth our while. You promised a lot more than that."

"It's all under control," Billy explains. "Them boys're strengthening the decks so we can take more."

"How many?"

"Maybe a thousand." Billy glances at Mason who shrugs unhappily. "Maybe more."

"That's more like it," Heath says. "I want at least a thousand. Force in as many as you can."

Heath pulls a gold pocket watch out and consults it. "It's past ten now. The trains are on their way to Camp Fisk. I want this vessel out of here by dark tonight, so I suggest, Mr. Sharp, that you and your partners hurry back to the camp and organize loading the trains. If anyone questions you, refer them to me. And remember, the more men on board, the happier I shall be."

"Yes, sir," Billy says as Heath turns and strides away.

"Cap'n Mason, the first train'll be here by two this afternoon," Billy says. "You'll be ready to load?"

Mason looks uncertain, but he nods.

"Excellent. Come on, boys. We got work to do."

As I follow Billy and Sam back to the wagon, my mind is reeling with questions, but I'll ask later. Right now, I'm happy. Whatever Billy, Sam, Mason and Heath have planned, it means I am going home and the journey will begin tonight. A few days on the river up to Cairo in Illinois and then a couple more on the train. I could be at the fishing hole on the farm in a week.

TWENTY-ONE

"**G**oddamn. It's too many. Do you want us all to end up at the bottom of the river?" Every deck of the *Sultana* is dark blue with men, and Mason isn't happy.

"Everything's fine." Billy's at his smoothest and most persuasive. "This is the last chance. Camp Fisk's empty now. There ain't goin' to be any more shiploads goin' north. Think of it this way. All you got to do is get this boat up to Cairo, Illinois, and we'll all be rich. Five dollars a head's nothin' to be sneezed at."

"More like three after you and Heath's taken your cut," Mason says sullenly.

"Look." Billy's voice becomes harder. "You can take it or leave it. We spent the day bringin' three trainloads of these boys down here from Fisk and we ain't about to take them back. Ain't no problem findin' other cap'ns who'll be more'n happy to take the government's money. Your choice: get the men off this boat or fire up the boilers and let's make some money."

Mason hesitates, glancing nervously round at the mass of men standing almost shoulder-to-shoulder on the upper deck. Most of them are painfully thin, and there's barely enough room for them to lie down to sleep, but every one has a smile on his face—they're going home.

"Very well, but it'll be slow going against the current, and I don't want to strain the boilers."

"Take all the time you want." Billy's smiling again. "Just get us to Cairo."

Mason grunts and heads toward the bridge to give orders for setting off. Billy and I thread our way back through the mass of men to join Sam at the stern rail.

"You know, Jake," Billy says with a laugh when we're settled, "sometimes I think money's a more powerful persuader than the old blade."

The afternoon, loading and unloading the trains, has been so busy I haven't had a chance to think about all the things that are worrying me. Now I have something new to think about.

"What did Mason mean about your cut?" I ask.

"Oh, that." Billy waves his hand dismissively. "It ain't much compared to what Mason and Heath is gettin', but if the government's throwin' money around, I don't see why I shouldn't have some. And you and Sam too, of course."

"That's why you want to cram as many men onto the *Sultana* as possible, it means more money for you?"

"And fer you," Billy says. "And Sam, of course. Sam here's goin' to spend his share on a set of wooden toes and a new pair of shoes, right, Sam?"

Sam laughs. "Right, Billy. Mind you, I might just save a few dollars for whisky and the ladies."

"And so you should," Billy agrees. "We earned a bit of recreation, I reckon. What'll you spend your cut on, Jake?"

"I don't want a cut," I blurt out.

Billy looks at me hard. "You're entitled," he says. "We're partners."

"Not anymore," I say. I haven't thought out a speech; I'm just saying what comes into my mind. "As you said, we aren't in Andersonville anymore. I'm not proud of what you—we—did in there to survive, but that's past now. I appreciate all you did for me in Andersonville, but I want to get back to my old life without stealing and killing."

I fall silent. Billy continues to stare at me, and Sam looks from one of us to the other, to see where this will go.

"I al'ays knew we was from different worlds, Jake, boy. I reckon we needed each other in Hell, but we ain't there anymore."

Billy laughs suddenly and slaps me on the shoulder. "We had some times though, didn't we?"

I nod. Sam relaxes visibly.

"Well, I know what I'm doin' with my money," Billy says. "I aim to head for the city, find myself a little place and get a regular job."

"Regular job?" Sam asks. "I can't see you tending store."

"Why not?" Billy asks. "I reckon I'd make a fine storekeep."

"You have your hand in the pickle jar too much to make any money," Sam jokes.

"You might be right there," Billy says. "But I ain't thinking on keepin' store. Man in Vicksburg told me the Pinkertons are movin' out of spyin' now that the war's over. Settin' themselves up in law enforcement, I hear. Huntin' down all them boys as figure to use what they learned in the war to relieve banks and trains of a little extra cash. Now there's somethin' I know about, least one side of it. Reckon that'd be useful learnin' in that line of work."

I nod tiredly. I'm glad I've made the break with Billy, but I'm exhausted. It's been a hectic day. Fortunately, everybody is so keen to go home they did exactly what they were told. The only complaints were from some men on the third train when they saw how crowded the *Sultana* already was. But they went on board anyway. The urge to get home and leave the war behind is too strong. Still, I'm nervous.

"Do you think Mason is right about the overcrowding?" I ask.

"He's an old woman," Billy dismisses the captain. "To make somethin' of yourself you got to take chances. Sure, she's overcrowded, but she'll be fine."

"But the *Sultana*'s got six times as many passengers as she's licensed for."

"Look, Jake, you just lost the right to question me. *Sultana*'s still floatin'. It'll be a slow journey, but's not like we're headin' out to sea. We're on the Mississippi River."

"I guess so."

"I know so. Now let's get us as comfortable as we can."

In any case, it's too late to do anything about it. Dark smoke is belching out of the *Sultana*'s huge funnels, and amidst a chorus of shouted orders, lines are being untied and gangplanks pulled in. The giant paddle wheels begin to grind around and the *Sultana* edges away from the dock.

"Hey!" A voice shouts from the dockside rail. "There's one of them photographer fellas, wants to take picture of all us returning heroes."

A ripple passes across the packed deck as men push to the rail to see what's going on. The *Sultana* lurches sickeningly over. Above us, in the middle of the boat, Mason hurls the bridge door open and screams at the crowd, "Get back, you idiots. Do you want to capsize us?"

No one listens. Billy laughs. There's too much excitement. We're like a bunch of children returning from a day out.

I'm excited too. But I can't ignore the knot of foreboding that's settling in the pit of my stomach.

TWENTY-TWO

"**Y**ou worry too much, Jake. I told you everything would be fine. We've been two days and nights on the river and, apart from the lurches when everyone rushes to rubberneck at the passin' sights, it's bin a breeze."

Billy's right. It's been uncomfortable and slow, but nothing has gone wrong. We've even had a chance to stretch our legs in Memphis before we left at midnight, a full two hours ago. I've almost got used to the lurches. Not all are due to the passengers moving from side to side. The current against us is strong and sometimes, when we are rounding a bend in the river, it catches us sideways and we tilt over quite dramatically.

Since we left Vicksburg and I told Billy we weren't partners anymore, I haven't seen much of either him or Sam. Earlier today in Memphis, they went ashore together and arrived back just as the gangplank was being pulled in. Billy came running from town and had to shout at the sailors to keep the gangplank in place while Sam hobbled down the street. They were both laughing uproariously.

I wouldn't be talking to Billy now, except there was something worrying me and I could think of no one else to talk to.

"I was talking to a crewman this afternoon when we docked at Memphis," I went on.

"And he told you the *Sultana's* overloaded," Billy scoffed. "Everybody says that, but here we are, near two hours past Memphis."

"Well, yes, but he said something else. The overcrowding on the top decks makes the *Sultana* top heavy."

"Yeah," Billy says dismissively. There was not even a pretense that we were friends in his tone of voice. "That's why she lurches so. I know that."

"But," I doggedly keep going, "he also said that these steamboats aren't designed to lean over like the *Sultana* does. The four boilers are connected, so when

160

she leans to the right, the water from the two left-hand boilers pours into the right-hand boilers."

"So?"

"That means that the bottoms of the partly empty left boilers heat up too much. He says you can see the plates glowing red hot."

"You're gettin' a bit technical for me here. What're you tryin' to say?"

"When the *Sultana* rights herself again," I continue patiently, "the water pours back to the left, hits the overheated boiler plates and boils."

"Ain't that what's supposed to happen in boilers?" Billy asks sarcastically.

"Yes," I say with as much patience as I can muster. "But with the plates being too hot, the water boils too fast. That increases the pressure in the boilers. The opposite happens when she lurches to the other side."

"You talk to a sailor for ten minutes and suddenly you're an expert on ship's boilers." Billy sounds annoyed.

"But the boilers aren't in good shape. They were repaired in Vicksburg, and they've got weak patches on them. You heard the man report to Mason on the dock before we sailed. The sailor told me that he would give all his pay for this journey just to make it to Cairo."

"Well, he can give it to me when we get there," Billy snaps. "I'm becomin' a might tired of your whinin', Jake. Like I said, we been on the river for two days and nothin's gone wrong. Nothin's gonna go wrong in the next two. You want no part of this riverboat deal, so be it, but don't come complainin' to me. You got a problem, go see Mason and leave me alone. I aim to get me a few hours sleep."

Billy turns his back on me and stretches out on the deck.

I don't feel like sleeping. Picking my way between the snoring bodies, I work my way forward until I am just back of the smokestacks. I lean on the rail and look out over the water. Should I go and talk to Mason? What good would it do? He's the captain; he must know what's going on at least as well as any sailor. Either the boilers are not the problem the sailor suggested or Mason is ignoring it. Whichever it is, I won't change his mind.

It's a beautiful night with a clear sky and the sliver of a new moon. We are passing the low black shapes of some small islands and entering a long sweeping curve. We're making heavy going against the strong current; below me I can hear the thump of the engines straining to turn the giant paddle wheels.

I envy Billy. He doesn't care about anything or anybody. That must make life easy. I worry about the boilers, and Nathaniel's ghost still haunts my dreams. Not as often as before, but when I least expect him, there he is, asking me why I didn't save his life. Why should I care? He'd be dead by now whatever I had done.

I shake my head and curse quietly into the darkness. Perhaps the problem isn't Nathaniel. Perhaps it's my brother Jim.

I volunteered for the army to take Jim's place, to be like him. Jim would never have allowed Billy to stab Nathaniel. He always protected the weak, and he would have fought to save the poor fool, even if it was pointless. But more than that, I can't help thinking that my relationship to Jim was very like Nathaniel's relationship to me. I must have seemed weak and annoying to Jim, but he never showed it, and he helped, protected and taught me whenever he could. Nathaniel followed me around just like I did with Jim, but I just pushed him away and, at best, let him die.

I curse again. Half of me wants to be uncaring, like Billy. The other half wants to care too much, like Jim. Why does it have to be so damned complicated?

"Admiring the view?" Sam steps up and leans on the rail beside me.

"Something like that," I say.

Sam belches loudly, and I smell the sour odor of cheap liquor on his breath. I remember he was carrying a jug when he and Billy came back on board.

"Shoulda come 'shore with us," Sam slurs. "Good t'get solid ground 'neath your feet. No pickin's though. Not like Vickshburg."

"Pickings?"

"Shure. Memphish's not like Vickshburg. That woman was easy. Tap on the back of the head and whoosh, off comes the necklash. Had to hit the fella harder though. Nice watsh. Good pickin's."

I realize that Sam's telling me about the necklace that Billy bribed Heath with. "Did you kill them?" I ask.

"Naw. Don't think so, any rate. Shouldn'ta bin walkin' 'lone at night. Own fault. Hada good stack o' cash on 'im though. Heath never saw that. I'm gonna go sleep now."

Sam turns away but I grab his arm. "You robbed those people in Vicksburg to get us on the *Sultana*?"

Sam looks suddenly worried. "Ain't gonna tell Billy I told you, are you? He said fer me not to say. Says that you was lily-livered and not up to doin' the work proper."

I'm suddenly angry. Billy's been playing me for the fool ever since I first met him. On some level I realized that, but in Andersonville I had persuaded myself that the normal rules didn't count, that I had to do whatever was necessary to survive. Well, I'd survived and now I face a choice. Do I go on turning a blind eye to Billy, Sam and their kind, or do I do something about it?

I push Sam away and head toward the back of the boat. I don't know what I'm going to say when I find Billy, but I'm certain I have to do something.

Sam stumbles along behind me. "Your not gonna tell Billy, are you?" he whines pathetically. I ignore him.

TWENTY-THREE

"Dammit, watch where you're going."

The *Sultana* is leaning over as she struggles around the bend, making me stagger and trip over the tightly packed sleeping bodies. Even though I am now farther from the paddle wheels, the noise of the engines sounds louder, as if they are straining extra hard. I imagine the water sloshing into the boilers on the low side of the boat, just like the sailor told me.

With startling speed, the *Sultana* rolls back onto an even keel. I lose my footing completely, kicking another sleeping figure who curses loudly. I only manage to keep my feet by wrapping my arms around a vent that rises from the deck. I glimpse Sam waving his arms about as he tries to keep his drunken balance on the tilting deck.

The first explosion is more of a dull roar. It originates deep within the *Sultana* and rises somewhere back where Sam and I were standing. The roar gains volume until I am deaf from the tortured sounds of twisting metal and shattering wood.

Then there's an almost uncanny silence that seems to last forever but can be no more than a second or two. I cling to the vent and am vaguely aware of figures moving around me. Sam is nearby. "What'n hell?" he says.

The second explosion is much louder than the first. It begins with a boom, like a large cannon firing nearby, and is followed by the wail of tearing metal. A ball of fire leaps into the air, turning night into day. I look up and see black shapes, some recognizably human, twisting in the red glow.

The flames are followed by a white cloud of superheated steam that races along the exposed deck. Pain sears the backs of my hands where they cling around the vent, but the rest of me is protected. Men are screaming all around me. I slump down into a huddle. Above me flaming coals arc like a madman's insane fireworks display, and lumps of wood, metal and human bodies curve away and splash into the illuminated water.

I look down at my burned hands. They don't hurt now, but the backs are an angry red and whitish blisters are already forming. Gradually, I become aware of shadowy figures around me. Some stand still, and others stumble around helplessly. Quite a number are climbing the ship's rail and jumping into the water.

One figure is close by, sitting with his hands over his face mumbling what sounds like, "Ine glinde," over and over again. His feet are bare and he has no toes.

I reach out and touch Sam's shoulder. He drops his hands and turns his head. I scream. Sam's face is gone; all that is left is a raw mass of scalded flesh. His eyeballs have melted. The black hole where his mouth used to be moves. "Ine glinde," it says. I scramble around the vent away from the horror.

The deck ends in a ragged edge of shattered wood about twenty feet in front of me. If I hadn't decided to go and confront Billy, I would have been there. I crawl over and look down.

The explosions have torn the *Sultana*'s heart out. A huge hole, fringed by a tangled mass of twisted machinery and charred beams, has replaced the space between the paddle wheels where the boilers used to be. Fires rage out of control in several places and grow together as I watch. The screams of those still alive and trapped in the inferno are agonizing.

One deck below on the far side, the wall has been ripped away from a cabin. The bed hangs at a crazy angle over the abyss, but the rest of the furniture is untouched. Even the water jug and basin sit in the sideboard, ready for use. A woman and her daughter, both with striking blonde hair, stare in horror out over the wreckage while a man with dark hair struggles to force the cabin door open. I notice the girl is wearing a red nightdress.

I feel oddly sorry for the family. I'm a soldier. I've been in battle and I've been in Hell. Violence is part of my life, but not this family. They represent innocence and the world I am trying to get back to. They shouldn't have to be a part of this.

Silently wishing the family luck, I push myself away from the edge and retreat to the stern. By the time I have fought my way there, the entire center section of the *Sultana* is in flames and the fires are moving toward me. People are climbing the rail and leaping into the dark water all around. I think of the hopeless soldier in Andersonville crossing the dead line. The *Sultana's* rail will be a dead line for most of those who jump.

I mumble thanks to Jim for teaching me to swim when we were boys.

The water around us is lit up as bright as day by the fire. It is filled with floating bodies, struggling figures and debris. Here and there, a few men cling to timbers or pieces of decking.

"Where the hell's Sam?" I turn to see Billy pushing through the mass of bodies toward me.

I shake my head dumbly, too stunned to speak.

"What the hell happened?"

"The boilers," I manage to croak out. "I told you."

"What? Oh yeah. Well, ain't nothin' we can do about it now. Goddammit. Government ain't gonna pay for dead men on a lousy ship that blew up. I was aimin' to set myself up with that money."

"Goddamn you, Billy," I scream. Hundreds of men are dead or dying because of Billy's, Sam's, Heath's and Mason's greed, and still all Billy can think of is his lost money. I turn away in disgust.

The fire is approaching with frightening speed, eating its way along the tar-soaked decking. The crush of people around us is increasing as those who can't or don't want to jump from the rail crowd as far back as possible. I can feel the heat on my face and am aware of a growing pain in my raw, blistered hands.

Billy grabs my arm. "Where's Sam?" he repeats.

"Dead," I say. I don't know if he is yet, but he will be soon. No one can survive the injuries I saw.

"So it's just you and me again, Jake, boy. Just like Andersonville. We stick together, remember? Organize, that's the way to survive."

"Go to hell," I say. The thought of Billy and his arrogant self-interest makes me sick. I refuse to be drawn back into the twisted world of Andersonville.

I try to shake off Billy's grasp, but his grip is tight and the crush of people around us doesn't allow me any purchase.

"What're you doin', Jake?" There's a note of panic creeping into Billy's voice. "We got to stick together."

I try to shake him off again, but he pulls me around and grabs me with his other hand. He pulls me close, almost embracing me now. I struggle, but my hands are agony and the crush of people doesn't allow me to get away. Billy thrusts his mouth close to my ear. His voice is a scared, high-pitched whine.

"Jake, don't leave me. I don't want to burn."

"Then jump," I say coldly.

"For pity's sake, Jake. I can't swim."

Billy pulls back and looks at me. His eyes are darting back and forth, and beads of sweat are running down his face. All pretence at arrogance is gone, replaced by sheer terror.

Billy gulps convulsively. "I ain't never been this feared, Jake, boy. Help me."

I feel no pity for Billy. "This is how Nathaniel felt the night you stabbed him," I say harshly.

Billy looks confused for a minute; then he remembers. "I didn't mean that, Jake. I got carried away. I'm sorry."

I sigh. I don't believe a word Billy's saying about being sorry, but it's not my place to judge him. The man in front of me is just a pitiful, helpless human being. Exactly the sort of person my brother Jim would help. Judgment is for later, if there is a later.

"All right," I say. "My hands are burned. Hold on to my arm and don't let go."

I lead Billy over to the rail. People are jumping all over now. The main danger is going to be a jumper landing on us when we're in the water.

"When we jump," I tell Billy, "it's important that we get as far from the side of the boat as possible."

Billy nods. We climb the rail and put one foot on top. Billy's grip on my arm is like a vice.

"The water will be cold, but just hold on. We'll come back to the surface."

Billy's breathing heavily. It looks a long way down, and the water below looks very crowded.

"Don't let me go, Jake," Billy says, forgetting that it's him holding onto me. "I can't swim. I don't want to drown. I'm scared."

"Shut up," I say, and we jump.

TWENTY-FOUR

The shock of cold water forces me to cough a bubble of air out. We sink a long way. I can feel the river current tugging at us. Billy is almost ripping my arm off. Wildly, I try to swim with my free arm. My hands are in agony. In the glow from the fire above I can see pale ghost-like strips of skin coming off them as I move. Are we sinking or floating?

My head breaks the surface beside the body of a sailor. He's wearing a crude cork lifejacket. I gasp, frantically hauling air into my tortured lungs. Billy kicks me hard on the leg. He's clinging onto my arm with both hands and wildly kicking to try and stay afloat. All he does is drag us under again.

"Let go! You'll drown us both," I scream as we surface a second time.

Billy ignores me. He's in a complete panic, both his arms wrapped tightly around my left arm and his face only a few inches from mine. His eyes are wild and he's jabbering incoherently. We go down a third time.

When we come up, I throw my free arm over the floating body, lean back and head butt Billy in the face as hard as I can. I think I hear the crack of his nose breaking, but the sudden pain makes his eyes focus and stare into mine.

"You'll kill us both," I yell. "Loosen your grip or I'll hit you again."

Billy looks stunned. He's gasping for air and keeps taking mouthfuls of water and coughing it back up. A stream of dark blood is running from his nose into his mouth and the river.

"I won't let you drown," I say as reassuringly as possible.

Billy's grip loosens.

"Hold onto the body," I order. "Kick your legs slowly to keep afloat."

Billy does as I tell him. The body sinks noticeably; the life jacket won't keep all of us up. I tread water to help, but the body won't float for long with our added weight. We have to find something better. Already my legs are aching.

I look around. The current has carried us away from the *Sultana*, which is now a raging inferno. Dark shapes, limbs flapping like broken puppets, leap from any area of deck that is not on fire. The screams of those trapped in the burning wreckage echo across the water.

Hundreds of bodies bob hopelessly on the water. Those still alive struggle to stay afloat or cling to whatever piece of wreckage they can. Three men, sitting apparently comfortably on a wide piece of decking, drift by. I spot something, a door, I think, low in the water about thirty feet away.

"Billy, we can't stay here."

Billy's eyes widen with fear. "I ain't lettin' go."

"You won't have to," I say calmly. "There's a door over there. Just do as I say and we'll swim over to it. Hold the body lightly and kick your legs like this." I show Billy what to do.

Progress is painfully slow, and Billy keeps pushing the body down and swallowing water, but we gradually get closer.

When we are only about ten feet from the door, I notice someone on the far side of it, a dark-haired man and a blonde girl. He is desperately trying to get her onto the door, but he's too weak and the door keeps tipping up and sliding her off.

"Help me," the man says as we reach the door. "For pity's sake, look after my daughter. I have to find my wife."

Billy grabs the edge of the door gratefully. It tips dangerously. I grab the daughter's red nightdress and haul as the man pushes from the other side. The girl moves her arms, trying to help, but she's too weak to be any use.

At last we get her stable on the door. Everything is fine as long as she stays still and Billy doesn't panic.

"Look after her," the man says. "I have to find my wife."

"Stay," I say. There's no chance of finding his wife, even if she's still alive, in this chaos. The man ignores my plea, lets go of the door and swims off among the floating debris.

The girl looks at me and smiles weakly. I doubt she has the strength to move. "Thank you," she whispers. I look at the blonde hair and red nightdress and realize it's the girl I saw in the cabin after the explosion. Her father succeeded in getting his family out. I hope he finds his wife.

The door lurches wildly as Billy tries to climb onto it. The girl clings on and whimpers in fear.

"Stop it," I shout.

"Got to get up," Billy says. "Got to get out of the water." At least he's stopped clambering and the door is stable again.

"It's not big enough," I explain. "If we try to get on, it'll tip over and we'll all drown."

"Then push the girl off," Billy says. "She's almost dead already, and I can't swim."

I look at the girl. She's eleven or twelve years old. Her eyes are wide with fear, and blue, like Nathaniel's.

"No," I say, turning back to Billy. "She stays on the door."

"We've al'ays stuck together, Jake. Haven't we?" Billy's voice takes on a wheedling tone. "She ain't gonna last the hour, and I can't hold on much longer. You don't want to see your pal Billy drowned for a stranger who's dyin' anyway. Do you?"

"I don't want to see you drown, Billy, but I'm not pushing that girl off. She has as much right to a chance to live as you or me. If we hold onto the door, we'll be all right until help arrives."

Billy lunges at the girl. I've been half expecting it, and I grab his arm before he gets a hold of her.

Pain shoots up my arm from my burned hand, but I pull Billy's arm away. The girl tries to sit up and the door lurches wildly. Billy loses his grip and flails his arms frantically. I can't hold him anymore; the pain in my hand is too much. I let go.

The girl has managed to stay on the door, and I hook my elbows over the edge to help steady it. By the time I look around, Billy is four or five feet away. He's waving his arms in a strange mockery of swimming, but all it's doing is tiring him.

"Billy!" I yell. "Calm down."

It's no use. He's shouting something, but he keeps swallowing mouthfuls of water, so I can't make out more than a few words, "help," "Jake," "drown," "pals."

I want to let go of the door, swim over to Billy, calm him down and bring him back, but I know I can't. I could possibly reach him but I don't have the strength to bring him back, and my hands aren't much use anymore. Besides, the door is drifting faster than Billy, and the distance between us is increasing every moment that I hesitate.

I shout advice to Billy. "Stop waving your arms." "Kick your legs slowly." But all I'm doing is trying to convince myself that I'm doing something useful.

Eventually, Billy stops struggling. Only his face is above the water, and every small wave washes over it. I see his mouth moving, but I can't hear him anymore. Then he's gone.

TWENTY-FIVE

And then one morning there were no guards. We just walked out the gates. Don't know what we'd have done if the cavalry hadn't showed up. Just wandered, I guess."

The girl in the red nightdress on the door hasn't said anything for a long time, but I'm still talking to her. I've told her about Jim and the fishing hole; about Jim getting killed and me joining up; about Cold Harbor and Andersonville. Of course I haven't told her everything; people who haven't been to Hell shouldn't have to know what goes on there.

At first I talked to keep her spirits up and keep her awake, but since she passed out I've been talking for myself. It seems to help to say the story out loud.

As far as I can tell, we've been in the water about an hour. The cold has numbed me so much my hands don't even hurt anymore.

We've drifted a long way. The *Sultana*, or what was left of her, ended up on one of the small islands we passed. She was still burning when we drifted round the bend in the river and I lost sight of her.

There are not many people in the water now. Most of the bodies have sunk and many of the fittest have made it to shore or onto one of the islands. Occasionally I see a figure in the gloom clinging to something that floats, but they are just rough shapes.

A wave tilts the door, and I grab the girl to stop her from sliding into the water. I don't even know if she's still alive. I hope so, otherwise none of this is worth it and she'll just be another ghost to join Nathaniel, Sam, Billy and Jim in my dreams.

"Here's another." It takes me a moment to realize that the voice isn't in my mind. Very carefully, so as not to upset the door, I turn my head. The side of a ship rises like a wall frighteningly close, its rail lit by burning torches above my head. How did it get here without me noticing? I must be worse off than I think.

Two sailors, attached to the ship by ropes, jump into the water and swim over.

"You'll be all right now," one of them says.

"The girl," I wheeze.

One of the sailors swims around the door and examines her.

"Ain't nothing we can do for her," he says. "She's dead. Let's get you on board."

"No," I say as loudly as I can. "Take her first."

"No point," the sailor says. "She ain't breathing."

"Take her first or I don't go." The effort of shouting at the sailor exhausts me, but it's vitally important that I do everything I can. There have been too many deaths.

"Another crazy one," the second sailor says. "If it'll make him come easy, take her on board first."

I watch to see that they get the girl on board, and then I black out.

⸺⸱⸺

The hospital bed is the most comfortable thing I have slept on since I left home. As I wake from my troubled dreams, I imagine that I am floating on feathers. I struggle awake and open my eyes. I see sunlight glaring off a white ceiling. Gingerly, I move my head to look around. I'm in a long ward with beds packed tightly down both sides. The man to my left is almost totally covered in bandages. Tall windows let in a low sun, but I can't tell whether it's morning or evening. I move my hands and gasp with the pain.

"Good morning." I turn my head to my right to where the voice is coming from.

"You've been out for two days. Thought you were never going to wake up." The speaker is the man in the bed to my left. He's sitting, propped up on pillows, and smiling at me.

"You from the riverboat that blew up?"

"Yes," I answer.

"I saw them working on your hands. They burned?"

"Yes." Gently I lift my arms until I can see the huge bundles that are the bandages over my hands.

"Lot of burns came in the last few days. Some a lot worse than hands."

"What's wrong with you?" I ask. The man's annoying me. I don't want to talk. And he looks fine.

"What's left of me's in good shape." The man looks down his bed. My eyes follow and I notice for the first time that the bulge of his body under the blankets stops below the waist.

"I'm sorry."

The man shrugs. "My own stupid fault. I was working in the rail yards back at the turn of the year. It'd been snowing and I slipped under a train. Took my legs off clean as you like. Still, I was lucky. There was a doctor on the train, knew how to stop the bleeding. Been up and down though with fevers and such. Given me up for dead more times than I like to think, but it ain't my time yet, I reckon. Yours neither by the looks of things.

"They say more than sixteen hundred went down with the *Sultana* and plenty others are dying every day in this very hospital. Fellow on the other side of you won't last long either."

Sixteen hundred. I roll back and stare at the ceiling. Billy, Sam, Captain Mason, the family from the cabin. The thought of the girl in the red nightdress brings tears to my eyes. I know I did everything I could, but while I was in the river, I couldn't shake the idea that saving her was my salvation too. Somehow it would make up for all that I had done. But she was dead. I'd failed again.

I look back at my neighbor. I can't take my eyes off the flat blanket where his legs used to be. At least my hands will heal.

"We make a great pair, huh?" the man says. "Me with no legs and you with bum hands.

"I know what you're thinking," he continues. "It's what everyone thinks when they see me. You're thinking that, apart from some scars, your hands'll heal. All this poor cripple can look forward to is life sitting in a chair or pushing himself around on a wheeled trolley. And you'd be right.

"To be honest, I ain't looking forward to it, but seeing your eyes, I'd say you've got worse scars than me. The scars you carry ain't just on your hands. And if you carry them inside scars with you, they'll cause you more grief than my missing legs."

I roll back and wish he would shut up. Are my troubles so obvious that everyone can see them as easily as if I were carrying a sign? To my great relief the man beside me stops talking and I eventually drop back to sleep.

JUNE 1865

TWENTY-SIX

I hesitate at the foot of the bed. I want to leave. I want to go home, but it's not easy. The five weeks of rest and food in the hospital have worked wonders. I almost feel human again. My hands are almost healed, and it's been a long time since I screamed when the doctor changed the dressings. I'll even miss my talkative, legless neighbor. As soon as I walk out that door at the end of the ward, it'll be just me and my ghosts. And I have a new one now. As I suspected, the girl in the red nightdress has joined the others in my nighttime accusations.

I've tried to find out what happened to the girl and her family after we were pulled onto the boat. I've asked everyone I can, but there's no blonde girl in a red

189

nightdress in this hospital or any of the other hospitals in Memphis. I don't know enough about her parents to even begin to search for them. It's hopeless. The girl and her parents are dead. Everyone I touch dies.

"Looks like you got visitors." It takes me a moment to realize that the legless man is talking to me. I turn toward the door. Who would come and see me?

Coming toward me down the ward, smiling broadly, are a woman and a girl. The girl's not wearing a red nightdress, but I would recognize her anywhere. My legs go weak with shock. Ghosts, I think. But everyone else can see them.

"Are you Mr. Jake Clay?" the woman asks.

I can't talk. I nod stupidly.

"I'm so glad we've found you at last," she goes on, holding out her hand. She hesitates when she sees the angry red scars on the backs of my hands. "My name's Annabelle Fletcher and this is my daughter, Sarah. We wanted to thank you for saving Sarah's life on the river."

"You're dead," I say, staring at the girl.

"Very nearly," the mother says. "The sailors on the *Bostonia* who pulled you both out of the river thought she was. Fortunately, there was a doctor as a passenger on board who was tending to the victims. He noticed that she was still breathing, but only just. He wrapped her in blankets and took her to his cabin. When the *Bostonia* reached Memphis, he took her to his home, and he and his wife nursed her back to health."

"Your husband found you?" I ask, looking from one to the other, still trying to take in what is happening.

"I'm afraid not." The woman's face darkens with sadness. "They found Joe's body on an island near where the disaster happened.

"I was picked up by a boat from Memphis. When Sarah was well enough to give the doctor details, he came looking and found me in a hospital on the other side of town. All she could talk about was the man who had talked to her on the river. So, we came looking for you."

I can think of nothing to say and continue to stare dumbly at them both.

"Well," the woman says eventually, "I'm very glad we found you before we caught the train home. You saved my girl's life, and I will always be grateful to you. If you pass though Boston, there will always be a welcome for you at our house."

She places a hand gently on my shoulder. "I wish you well and pray that your wounds heal completely. Thank you again."

"Thank you," the girl says with a sad smile. Then they are gone.

"I must say," the legless man comments, "you're quite the conversationalist once you get going." He chuckles quietly to himself. "You really save that girl's life?"

"Yes. I did," I say.

"Well, that's something to be proud of in this whole sorry mess, and no mistake."

He's right. I should be proud, and I will be, as soon as what has happened sinks in. I saved her life. At last, I have something positive to hold onto. Something I can remember when the blackness of the hell I've been through threatens to overwhelm me. Something that might just lay Nathaniel, Billy and the others to rest.

I nod to the legless man. "Take care of yourself."

"You too, Jake. Good luck."

I walk down the ward and out the door into the morning sunshine. I stop on the steps and look around. The world looks brighter and more colorful than I have seen it in months. A man walking past tips his hat to me.

"Morning," he says.

"Good morning," I reply. It's a statement as well as a greeting.

Perhaps I don't need to walk all the way home. I step after the man.

"Excuse me." He turns. "Which way is the railroad station?"

The man points down the street. "Take that wide road to the left. About half a mile. Can't miss it."

"Thank you."

I set off down the street. I can always walk the last bit if I need to, but I have to be sure and get home before the fall. There's a big old trout I have to catch.

JOHN WILSON is the author of twenty-three books for juveniles, teens and adults. His self-described "addiction to history" has resulted in many award-winning novels that bring the past alive for young readers. Incredibly, even the worst of the horrors that Jake experiences in *Death on the River* actually happened.